INFAMOUS

K.M. SCOTT

The emotional conclusion to Cade and Hailey's story that began in Notorious!

We tend to hurt the ones we love the most, even if we don't mean to. Cade March knows that all too well, and now Hailey does too.

For the first time in his life, he loves a woman enough to make things right. Whatever it takes, Hailey's worth it.

And for the first time in too long, she's willing to take a chance because what she feels when she's with Cade makes her truly happy.

But what happens if his past never goes away?

Infamous is a work of fiction. Names, characters, places, and events are the products of the author's imagination. Any resemblance to events, locations, or persons, living or dead, is coincidental.

2021 Copper Key Media LLC

Published in the United States

ISBN: 978-1-955335-00-3

CHAPTER ONE

ade

I LOOK DOWN IN HORROR AT KYLIE DOING HER whatever the fuck she's doing right near my zipper and see Taryn and her camera guy getting the whole thing to spread across social media. No, this can't happen. I don't know what Kylie's going for with this faux fellatio act she's got going on, but she needs to get the fuck up off my crotch right now.

"Enough!" I yell at her, but the crowd's too loud for her to hear anything.

Behind me, her sister tries to get her attention, begging her to stop. "Kylie! What are you doing? Stop this!"

Nothing seems to faze her, so I grab her ponytail and yank her head back roughly. She looks up at me with confusion written all over her face, like she can't understand why I'd be unhappy at this moment.

"Up. The show is over," I bark.

She doesn't fight me, and a second later, she's up on her feet taking a bow to the delight of the crowd in front of us that cheers and hollers for more. Taryn's right there when Kylie climbs down off the bar to interview her, although I can't imagine what she needs to ask her.

Maybe why, exactly, was she acting like pretend blowjobs are part of our job here? That sounds like a good question to start off with.

I glance out at the crowd and see Hailey staring up at me. What the fuck is she doing here? She's far enough away that she can't read my lips when I try to tell her this isn't what she thinks. What it is I'll need a hell of a lot more than a few mouthed words to explain, but I see in her eyes she can't believe what she's just watched.

Fuck!

Jumping down off the bar, I turn to look for Katelyn. She shakes her head like she's in shock at what her sister just pulled in front of the entire fucking crowd, but I don't have time to discuss that.

"I have to leave for a few minutes. Pry your sister away from the camera and you two handle things here," I snap, not interested in having any discussion with her.

"I'm so sorry, Cade. Kylie's been trying to get an audition—" she says, her eyes filling with tears as she attempts to give me an explanation for what her sister just did.

Pushing past her, I shake my head. "Not interested. Just take care of things and don't let it get to be a shitshow while I'm gone. I'll be back in a couple minutes."

My eyes dart left and right as I scan the crowd for any sign of Hailey. Too many people get in the way, and when I come around the corner of the bar where Taryn has been talking to Kylie, I feel someone's hand clamp down on my forearm.

"Cade, come talk to all my fans at Tampa Scene. After that show you two put on, I'm sure people want to know more about you," Taryn coos, like there's anything to fucking say about what just happened.

I tear my arm from her hold and flash Kylie a look that says I'm barely containing the rage inside me at this moment. "There's nothing to tell. It was all her."

She doesn't get a chance to say another word before I plow into the mob of people all jacked up from our little show. The music slams into me with every step I take, but I don't see Hailey anywhere. Damnit! I'm losing precious time to find her and explain everything.

Assuming she's even willing to give me a chance and listen to a goddamned word I have to say.

Right before I reach the door, someone grabs my arm to stop me, and I turn to see it's Alex. With a smile, he asks, "Hey, what the fuck was that all about up there?"

I throw him a look like I just gave to Kylie. "What

the fuck was that all about? A better fucking question is why the fuck Hailey was here, Alex. I didn't tell her about this tonight. Did you?"

Before he can answer my question, the sheepish look that comes over his face does it for him. I shove him away from me and force my way through more people to finally get to the door.

The warm night air hits me before I even step outside, and I run into the street to see if I can find her. She wouldn't have come alone, but she might drive her own car. I look for it, my gaze darting up and down the road searching for that white car of hers.

But I don't see it.

"Cade, she's gone by now," Alex says as he comes up behind me.

I spin around, livid and barely able to see straight as I stare at the person I know is responsible for this mess. "What the fuck was she doing here in the first place?"

That sheepish look from a minute ago is now full of regret as he winces like my goddamned question hurts him. When he doesn't answer me, I snap.

Pushing my hands against his shoulders, I send him flying back away from me. "What did you do? Why was she here tonight? Tell me!"

"I gave her friend Meadow V.I.P. tickets. I was hoping she'd swing by so she and I could have a drink and get to know each other more. I didn't think she'd invite Hailey. I swear, Cade. This isn't Hailey's kind of thing. I never thought she'd come with Meadow."

Every word just enrages me more, but when he gets to the part where he seems to think he knows anything about Hailey, I practically explode. "Why the hell do you think you know what Hailey's kind of thing is? You don't know her. You talked to her a couple times for like ten minutes tops. So that makes you some kind of goddamned expert on the woman I've been spending all my free time with? Don't act like you know what Hailey likes or what she's into because you don't know her."

Cash and Liam walk out of the club and come up behind Alex, stopping just as I finish barking at him. The two of them seem confused and look at one another and then me.

"What happened?" Cash asks in his calm way that at this moment makes me want to kill him.

I point at Alex in disgust. "Ask your fucking brother. He can tell you."

He and Liam focus on Alex, but he doesn't seem to have anything to say. I don't have the time to do what I want to do with him, so I push past all three of them and head back into the bar.

"What's wrong with him?" Liam asks as I walk by. "Does this have to do with the girl on the bar? Is that the one you were talking about, Alex?"

"No, it doesn't, but he can have her," I bark back at the three of them. "Feel free, Alex. She's ripe for the picking. Maybe then you can keep your nose out of my fucking business."

By the time I get back inside, I can barely keep my anger at bay. I should have stayed outside to cool down for another minute, but even a few more seconds being anywhere near Alex and I would have pounded the fuck out of him.

I see my father coming toward me through the crowd and know for damn sure the last thing I want to do is deal with him right now. Looking around for some escape, I head toward the back bar but see Maya standing there giving me a smug smile like she knows something terrible has happened to me tonight.

"Cade, where are you going? Why aren't you up at the front bar like you're supposed to be?" my father asks, yelling over the music and the ten or so people that separate us.

Fuck, I need some peace and quiet to think. Where the hell can I find that in this place? I see his office door, and as much as I don't want to have to talk to him, at least I'll be able to hear myself think for a moment or two before he comes charging in with his hundreds of questions I have no intention of answering.

I slip in and slam the door behind me, shutting out all that noise and all those people I can't handle right now. I need to find a way to talk to Hailey and explain what happened. I'd rather do it in person, but since I don't seem to have that option open to me at the moment, I'll have to take the next best thing and call her.

Her phone rings twice and then goes to voicemail. She's avoiding me. I try again and the same thing happens. A third time the call goes directly to voicemail.

Things are getting worse, not better. I could text her, but what I have to say doesn't belong in some bullshit message she'll probably delete as soon as she sees it's from me.

The office door opens, and the pounding music outside in the bar intrudes on my silence. I turn my head to look over at the door and see my father walk through, smiling like it's the best night of his life.

Good for him. My life is falling apart, but at least he's had a nice cash haul from the hundreds of drunks in attendance tonight.

"What a night, huh?" he says as he heads toward his desk. "That was some show you and Kylie put on. She's a real go-getter, that one."

"Yeah, real go-getter. Dad, I have something I have to deal with, so is it possible we could talk some other time?"

He looks up from the papers he's been shuffling around the top of his desk and nods. "Yeah, sure. Everything okay? Why aren't you out behind the bar?"

Always the job with him. Can't he tell I'm going through something right now? I just fucking told him I have something I have to deal with. Do I have to give him chapter and verse to find a little damn peace and quiet?

"Because I just said I have to handle something. Don't worry. I'll get back out there and pimp myself out for all the drunk women in a minute. In the meantime, the twins can manage the bar just fine. It's obvious Kylie has a grip on things tonight."

My father's expression morphs into one I rarely see from him. Concern. The usual look I get from him is a mixture of irritation and disappointment. Sometimes he mixes in disgust, for good measure.

But the way he looks now doesn't happen often with me. Ava gets that look, but that's because she's his little girl, the apple of his eye he's worried might be harmed by some jackass guy.

Someone like me. Or him.

"What's going on, Cade? You look like you're going to be sick. Are you okay?"

I look away because I can't explain that the last thing I am at this moment is okay. "I'll be fine. Just have something I need to figure out."

"Are you in trouble?" he asks quietly, like he's genuinely afraid the answer to his question is yes.

Shaking my head, even as I know I'm in trouble that I may not be able to get out of with Hailey, I give him my best bullshit smile all those people outside that door get. "Me? No. I'll be fine. Always am."

"Well, if you're not, let me know," he says with worry in his eyes.

I don't know why that makes me snap, especially since he said that with some genuine sincerity, but suddenly, I can't stop myself from laughing. "Why? What are you going to do? Ask the other twin to do her little dance behind me while Kylie does a second show for the crowd? Figure out some way I can help make this night the best one in the club's history?"

My father's eyes open wide in shock. "What is wrong with you tonight? It looked like you were having fun up there with Kylie. It's all a show anyway. Nothing is real about what you guys do out there. Nobody knows that better than you do. It's why you're such a natural at this."

I storm over to his desk and plant my palms on the top of it, leaning down so we're eye-to-eye. "I don't want to be a natural at this. Why can't you understand that? I didn't want Kylie doing her little thing, whatever the fuck that was, with me in front of the entire bar. I'm here to serve drinks and pretend I fucking like people as I do it, so I smile and do just that, but I never signed up for that shit she pulled out there."

My outburst stuns him for a few seconds. Leaning back in his chair, he nods like he understands and says, "Okay. That's fair. But honestly, Cade, how is that any different from what you used to do when you bartended last summer?"

He doesn't understand how much I hate thinking back to those days, so of course he'd ask that question. I regret nearly everything I did then. If I could blame it on being stupid, I would, but I can't.

I knew what I was doing and I loved it. Every fucking minute of it. And now, all I can do is cringe at those memories.

"It may not be different, but I am. I'm different," I say, hanging my head as the regret courses through me so hard it makes my body ache.

"Okay. Then don't do anything like that. We don't need any of it."

I see in my father's eyes he has no idea what I'm

talking about. How could he? What's happened with Hailey came out of nowhere and turned my life upside down so fast that I haven't had a chance to truly understand what's going on. I can't blame him for not knowing.

"Cade, what's wrong with you tonight? I'm not talking about what happened with Kylie. I mean what's really going on," he asks in that softer voice he's only ever used when I was a little boy and he thought I'd been hurt on the field or lost a big game.

I look up at him and wish I could tell him about Hailey. For one moment, I'd like not to be fighting my father on everything in my life. I can't, though. Not yet. I know as soon as I say something to him, he'll tell my mother and she'll tell my aunts, which means the rest of the family will know.

I'm not ready to share Hailey with them yet. I might not even have her to share after tonight, but if I can get her to forgive me for what she saw, I want to keep what we have to ourselves for a few days more.

"I'm okay, Dad. Thanks for asking. And thanks for letting me use your office for a few minutes to get my head together."

He smiles as if we've had some breakthrough between us. "Anytime. And Cade, if this is about a girl, the truth never fails. If you haven't tried being honest yet, see what happens with that."

I don't have a choice now. The truth is all I've got. I can only hope Hailey is interested in hearing it.

CHAPTER TWO

ade

TEN TEXTS OVER THREE HOURS FOLLOWED BY
another five when they didn't get me an answer have
me crossing into full-blown stalker territory. They also
leave me still unsure if Hailey will ever speak to me
again.

I want to tell her what happened and that it meant
nothing to me. I tried in the messages, but they didn't
do much other than make me spiral out of control for a
few hours as I attempted to tend bar and playact like I
was having the time of my life while the whole time all
I wanted to do was find Hailey and make her see how
sorry I am.

"Why don't you go to her house?" Alex suggests as
the last of the crowd trails out the doors to end the
night.

"I forgave you for your stupid move, dude. Suggesting I go to her house in the middle of the night tells me you want that ass kicking I threatened to give you earlier," I say, still pissed off at him.

"I didn't mean right now, for God's sake. I meant tomorrow morning before she goes to work."

As I start cleaning up behind the bar, I have to admit I have no idea where she lives. "One problem with that. I've never been to her house. I don't know where that is. So that's going to make the riding in on my white horse act difficult, don't you think?"

"Then go to the restaurant. You know she'll be there."

I nod at that idea, which seems logical, but that shows Alex doesn't really know Hailey. After what she told me about how she fell apart when she found that asshole boyfriend of hers in bed with another woman, I have no idea if she'll be at the restaurant in the morning.

My chest aches at the thought that I hurt her like that guy did. No, I didn't sleep with another woman, but I know what she went through and I know she hurts easily.

If only I had just told her the truth.

As that little nugget of reality settles into my brain, I shake my head. It wouldn't have mattered if she knew what I really do for a living or not. Seeing me standing up on top of a bar while Kylie dropped to her knees and played around with my pants would have hurt her no matter what amount of truth she had from me.

"I'll try the restaurant then. And if she won't talk to me, I'll just have to set up camp near her car until she comes out and has to see me."

Alex chuckles at my newfound attitude. "Nice. Stalker 101. I'm a little surprised you're like this with her, though, Cade. I thought you were more about playing than anything else when it comes to women."

I finish washing a glass and set it onto the mat below the bar. He's not wrong. I've always been more about playing at relationships than actually being in them. Everything needed to stay fun and light. As long as that happened, I loved being with someone.

And when it turned into something else and I had to be honest about things, that's when everything fell apart. Every time. Without fail. I'm nothing if not reliable in my failures.

"Hailey's different. Some people you don't play around with. Some people deserve more than that."

A slow smile lights up his face, and he shakes his head. "I can't believe you finally found someone who you can say that about. Wait till Liam hears he won the bet. I'm never going to live this down considering I'm your best friend."

I stop and study his expression, trying to understand what he's talking about. "You guys bet on my love life?"

"You know Cash. He'd bet on virtually anything, if given the chance. The four of us made a bet when you'd finally find someone who would force you to change your bullshit. I lost by about three years. Cash had you at twenty-five, I think. Liam said twenty-three, and Wilder said never. But you know how he is."

"When did this happen? Where was I when you were taking bets on my future happiness?" I ask, stunned but not really surprised since Cash will bet on anything and get everyone to join in.

"Fourth of July picnic out at Grandma's house. Remember Cash got a little buzzed and when we were talking about that girl he just broke up with, he got pretty defensive saying none of us were doing any better?"

"Dude, I'd remember us all betting on when I'd finally meet someone I cared for. I was drinking that night, but I wasn't as fucked up as you guys."

Alex shrugs, like all of this is so common in his life that he can't remember the details. "You left early after you and some girl had an argument on the phone. I think she was pissed you didn't bring her to the party. As if you ever do that."

I think back to that Fourth of July party out at the house and remember that fight. I can't even think of her name right now, but she was sure I was up to no good and didn't believe I was actually at my grandmother's house for a family get-together. I ended up leaving early, disgusted and not interested in celebrating anything after a half hour of trying to convince someone I didn't even love that I wasn't cheating on her or doing anything other than hanging out with my cousins.

"Nice. I can't trust any of you people, can I? What was the bet for?"

"Hundred bucks. No one was really willing to pony up much since I wasn't too confident it would ever happen but then went with twenty-six," Alex says with a smile.

"Well, I guess Liam gets three hundred now, assuming Hailey will ever speak to me again. Or is the whole bet just based on me caring for someone and not if she cares about me in return?"

Waving away my scolding, Alex grimaces at my potential misery. "Don't think like that. She's going to hear you out. She likes you. Trust me."

"Trust you? You got me into this mess," I say, shoving my hand against his shoulder.

"First, no I didn't. If you didn't lie to begin with, this wouldn't have been a problem."

I stop him before he can get to whatever he thinks is the second point he should make. "You can't imagine seeing one of the twins acting like she's about to go down on me would be okay with Hailey."

He thinks for a moment and nods. "Okay, granted that would have gone over badly. But it doesn't matter because she likes you. She has from the first day we all met. Just tell her the truth and don't fuck it up so she can give you another chance. And then don't fuck that up."

"You act like I intentionally sabotage things for myself," I say with a chuckle.

Alex doesn't bother to answer, instead just leveling his judgmental gaze on me. Fuck him. That's crazy. What kind of madman would deliberately ruin a good thing that makes him happy?

M<small>Y</small> STOMACH TWISTS INTO A TIGHT KNOT OF anxiety as I pull into the parking lot at Comfort Food. Hailey's car is parked on the side, like usual, so she's here. Now I just have to get her to listen to me so she can know the truth.

I take a look in the rearview mirror and silently give myself the pep talk I've recited since I opened my eyes this morning. "She just needs to hear the truth. That's all. Tell her the truth and it'll be fine."

None of that has truly sunk in as real yet, but I can hope.

Walking toward the front door, I'm not sure my legs are going to hold me up and my palms feel like someone's dipped them in warm water. I take a deep breath and push the door open to walk in, only to see her father glaring at me from behind the counter.

"You need to turn around and go back where you came from, son," he says in an ominously threatening tone.

Things are not starting out well.

"Is Hailey here? I was hoping to talk to her."

My voice sounds suspiciously like that time I brought my prom date home at four in the morning and lied to her parents that the car broke down. They didn't buy it then, and Hailey's father isn't taking too kindly to me right now, if his angry frown and eyebrows drawn in expression is any indication.

"Did you hear what I said? You need to go. Now."

I'm not getting anywhere with him, so I crane my

neck to look back toward the kitchen. If I can see her back there, I'll try to get her attention and bypass this whole angry dad thing in front of me.

He's not having any of that, though, and comes around the counter looking like a bull charging the red blanket in front of him. And I'm the damn blanket!

"Why are you still standing here when I told you to leave?" he barks in my face.

Well, I guess I don't have to wonder if he knows what happened. I doubt anything I can say is going to make him happy right now, but I figure it won't hurt to try.

"I just want to talk to Hailey and explain everything. It was all a misunderstanding. I swear. If I can just talk to her, she'll see that too and everything will be okay."

Anger flashes in his faded blue eyes, and for a moment, I'm not sure he's not planning to physically throw me out of his restaurant. I get ready for him to grab me by the collar, but then Hailey walks out of the kitchen and touches her father's arm to get his attention.

"Daddy, let me talk to Cade for a minute, okay?"

Her father doesn't budge for so long that I wonder if he intends on standing between us during our conversation. Finally, after what seems like forever having those blue eyes staring at me in utter disapproval, he steps aside.

"You just let me know if you need me, Hailey. I'll be right over here," he grumbles before walking back behind the counter.

My first real chance to see Hailey makes my chest ache just like it did last night when I thought about her being hurt by what she saw. Her beautiful blue eyes don't look at me with that glare of hatred like her father's have in them, though.

It's worse than that. In hers, I see nothing but sadness.

"What do you want, Cade? I have to get back to my work," she says in a flat voice devoid of emotion.

"I just wanted to explain about last night," I say quietly as I realize some of the restaurant's customers are listening to us talk.

Before she can say anything, like go away or I never want to see you again, I touch her arm and motion toward the door. "Can we talk outside?"

Pulling away from me, she shakes her head. "I don't think so."

"Please? I just want to tell you some things."

I see by the hurt in her eyes that she wants to say no, but she's kind and good, so she nods and gives me a chance. Now I just have to make sure I don't blow it.

We walk out the door and go around to the side of the building before we stop. She won't look at me now but instead stares down at the ground.

"I know what you saw last night upset you, and I don't blame you, Hailey. I swear I had no part in that. The other bartender just started doing things, and before I knew it, she was kneeling in front of me. I never wanted that."

Still refusing to look at me, she shakes her head and continues to stare at that damn grease spot on the concrete near her feet. "It doesn't matter. Last night just proved what I thought all along. You and I aren't right for each other."

Fuck, I can feel her already walking away from me before she takes a single step. It's like she's closed herself off and won't let me in anymore.

I touch her arm and try again to make her understand what happened on top of that bar was nothing she should care about. "I swear, Hailey. I don't know why she did that, but I didn't want her to. Honestly."

Finally, she looks up at me, and in an instant, I see so much pain in her eyes that I wish she hadn't lifted her head. "You lied to me, Cade. That's the problem. Not that girl doing that to you up on that bar."

Her words stun me. Kylie's fake porn act isn't why she's upset with me?

"You mean about working at Club X? I'm sorry about that too."

"I have to go now."

My hand tightens around her wrist in a desperate attempt to keep her there with me for even a few seconds more. "No, don't go yet. Please let me explain. I can explain everything. I swear."

Those beautiful blue eyes of hers fill with tears. "I don't need you to explain, Cade. As I said, I figured it out a long time ago. We don't belong together. I'm not a red Jag kind of girl. I'm not an infamous Cade March kind of girl. Now just go and leave me alone, okay?"

My heart sinks at every word that comes out of her

mouth, and when she pulls her arm from my hold, I stand there watching her walk away like I've lost everything I care about in the world. I don't know what to do.

I've never been at this point with a woman. Usually by now, I've checked out of the relationship and it's just a matter of time before whoever she is breaks up with me. It's a relief and I move on, like always.

Only this time I can't. I can't move on because I care about this woman.

So what am I supposed to do now?

CHAPTER THREE

*H*ailey

MY FATHER STOPS IN FRONT OF MY WORKSPACE AND lets out one of those sighs of his that says he has something on his mind. I know what he wants to talk about. Cade. It's just that I don't want to talk about him or anything about the last couple weeks I spent with him.

It hurts too much.

"So you know, he's sat out in my parking lot all day in that car of his. He hasn't left once, not even to go to the bathroom. He must have some soda bottle in there with him."

I look up and frown at the thought of that. "Nice, Dad. Don't worry about him. He'll go away when I leave in a couple minutes."

"You know, I did my best angry dad act when he came in. He didn't give up, though. That usually scares people off. At least it scared your sisters' boyfriends when I did it with them. Do you think I'm losing my touch?" my father asks, his sly smile giving away what he really thinks.

But I don't want to play this game with him right now.

"I don't think you're losing it, Dad. You still look like a terrifying guy when you do your angry dad shtick," I say as I clean up my area to leave.

"Nobody said anything about losing it. That makes me sound like I'm going crazy. I was merely wondering if I had gotten soft in my old age. That's it."

"I have to go, Dad. I'll see you later. I think I'm going to go for a drive."

When I turn to leave, he stops me and kisses me on the cheek. "Okay, honey. Whatever makes you happy."

I force a smile and walk to the back door in the semi-conscious state I've been in all day. I think Hector says something as I pass him, but I'm not sure. I'm a million miles away.

Actually, I don't know where I am exactly. Or how I feel. Or what I'm doing. All I know is I hate feeling this way.

Again.

Stepping out into the late afternoon sun, I shield my eyes from the brightness after being in the kitchen for so long, but I trip over a can the cooks use for their cigarettes and go tumbling toward the pavement. Right before I hit, I feel hands on me, and then a moment later, I'm standing face-to-face with Cade.

"Glad I was here to catch you. That could have been a nasty fall."

Instinctively, I pull away from him, hating that's what I feel about him now. "Thanks."

We stand there for a moment in horrible silence. Well, it's horrible to me because I don't want to go but I don't know what to say to him.

"Hailey, please talk to me. Or if you won't talk to me, say you'll listen to what I have to say. I waited all day for you to come out in the hope that you'll hear what I have to tell you."

I look into his dark eyes and see him pleading with them too. I swore not twenty-four hours ago to never let myself be lured in by those eyes and that body, yet here I am doing just that.

"What could you possibly have to say that would be okay now, Cade? You lied to me. You told me you ran a club, but I saw that's not true. Why didn't you tell me it's your father's club and you bartend?"

"Because I don't. Not until recently, that is. Well, that's not exactly true either."

I put my hand up to stop him before he goes any further. "You seem to have trouble with the truth. That's reason enough for me to say you should stop now. I need to go."

"That's not what I meant. I bartended at Club X last summer. I hated it. I don't know if I hated it because I had to work for my father or because I just don't like bartending, even if I seem to be good at it."

I can't stop myself from saying, "Well, from what I saw last night, you put on quite a show. You're a natural as far as I can tell."

A look of hurt settles into his face. "That's not what I usually do when I bartend. All I usually do is pour drinks for people and smile, even though behind the bar is the last place I want to be. I stopped working at Club X after the summer, but now I don't really have a choice so I went back last week."

As much as I don't want to be curious, I ask, "Why don't you have a choice? Does your father really need help because someone quit on him and he doesn't have a replacement?"

Cade shakes his head, that silent answer the only one I get for nearly a minute. When he finally begins speaking again, he sounds so different from every other time I've heard him talk—like he's defeated about something—that I can't help but feel bad for him.

"I don't have a job. I never have. I graduated from college over a year ago and haven't done anything since. That's the absolute and ugly truth, as much as I wanted to hide that from you."

In my mind, visions of his car, his condo, his jet skis flash like facts to once again dispute his version of the truth. "Then how do you have all the stuff you own? People who don't have jobs don't drive the kind of car you do, Cade. I thought you were going to tell me the truth. To be honest, this seems like a strange thing to lie about."

"I wish it was a lie. I don't have a job. I have a trust fund that gives me more money than I need. That's how I can afford the car and the condo and everything else."

None of this makes any sense, even though he looks sincere as he explains all of it. "People don't lie about being wealthy, Cade. Or is it that you knew I wasn't wealthy so you decided to hide it from me? Was that it?"

A tiny smile brightens his gloomy face. "You sound like Alex. He always asks me why I lie about not having a job. I don't know why I lie. The messed up part of all of it is I could manage Club X. Nothing would make my father happier. I think he could die the happiest man in the world tomorrow if I told him today that I'd take over the club. He literally wants nothing else from me."

I narrow my eyes in confusion, unsure why anyone would act the way this man does. "So you lie about something you could be doing but don't instead of actually telling the truth that you're wealthy and don't have to do that thing you don't want to do? Am I getting this straight?"

"Not exactly. As of last week, I have to do something or I'm cut off from my trust fund. The almighty Stefan March lowered the boom on me, I suspect to get me to come back to work at the club, so now I have to get a paying job or work for him. I chose to work for him, and that's what I was doing there last night."

For a few seconds, I don't know what to say. This all sounds ridiculous. Wealthy people don't lie about where they get their money, and trust fund guys certainly don't. Not that I know many of them. Or any, other than the one standing in front of me at the moment.

But it doesn't make any sense.

"Why should I believe you?" I ask, unable to be anything but that blunt right now.

Cade frowns and then lets out a heavy sigh. "Because all of it is the truth. We can drive over to the club right now and my father can vouch for every word I told you. Of course, that would mean my entire family would find out about us and I'm not sure you're up for that."

"Why? Are you ashamed of me because I don't have a trust fund like all of you?" I ask with as much defensiveness as I possess inside me.

He quickly grabs my hand, probably afraid I'm about to run away. He's not entirely wrong if he believes that. This whole conversation is making my flight instinct go haywire.

"No! That's not it at all. The problem with my family is once they find out about us, we're going to have to go to every picnic, barbeque, birthday celebration, and get-together they have, and trust me on this. My family knows nothing better than how to party."

"And you wouldn't want to do those things with me?"

He brings my hand to his mouth and lightly kisses my knuckles. "I was sort of hoping to enjoy it just being the two of us before the March and Jackson clan descends on us. I'm used to it since I've lived it my whole life, but it can be a little overwhelming."

"Oh. Have your other girlfriends told you that when you brought them around your family?" I ask, obviously fishing to find out how many there have been before me who met them all.

Cade shakes his head at my question. "I've never brought anyone around my family."

"Because they can be overwhelming?"

Again, he shakes his head, but this time he gives me a smile when he answers, "Because I never felt like that for anyone before."

"Before?"

"Before you."

"Oh."

He kisses the back of my hand again and smiles one of those Cade smiles that could charm the birds out of the trees. "I'm sorry I lied. And I'm sorry you saw what you saw last night. And I'm sorry for how I made you feel. I didn't mean for that to happen. I would never hurt you, Hailey. I swear."

God, I promised myself I wouldn't fall for his charms and give in, but now that I'm standing here and he's apologizing for everything under the sun, how can I run away? He sounds sincere. I want to believe him.

But a nagging thought remains, and I can't take him back until I ask about it.

"If that isn't what you usually do when you bartend, why did you do it last night?"

He blows the air out of his lungs in a whoosh as a sheepish look comes over him. "Okay, here's the absolute truth. I don't know for sure why Kylie jumped up on the bar, and I definitely shouldn't have gone up there to get her down. I think it had to do with the woman from Tampa Scene magazine being there with a camera guy. Kylie might have been playing it up for Taryn."

When he stops talking, I have a sense he isn't finished. "Okay. Is that it?"

Cade winces and then says, "I slept with Taryn last Easter. Taryn and her sister. It wasn't anything big and was over as quickly as it started. One weekend. That was it."

"And Kylie? Is she an ex too?"

Shaking his head, he waves his hand in front of him like he wants to erase that idea from existence. "No, no. No Kylie or her sister. I'm sorry I told you about Taryn and her sister, but I promised to tell you the truth. I'd really rather you not know that about me."

"That you took advantage of being a good looking man and had sex with women whenever you wanted? This isn't a shock to me, Cade. The only shock, actually, is that you would want to be with me after those women. I'm not exactly the jump up on the bar kind of girl."

Fear fills his eyes, and he holds onto my hand even tighter now. "You're exactly the kind of girl I want, though. None of that meant anything, and not just to me but to those women too. That's not who I am now, Hailey. I promise. I'm exactly the guy you thought I was before last night."

For the first time since all that happened, I give him a smile. "You don't have to worry. I'm not going to run away this time. And for the record, I didn't run away last night. Meadow and I were leaving when I saw you up on that bar."

"You didn't like the club? Too noisy and too crowded for you?"

"Actually, I think she saw you before I did and was trying to protect me. To be honest, though, right before we started to head for the door, I was thinking I would have preferred to be with you on your balcony looking at the stars instead of being plastered against all those people and not being able to hear myself think because the music was so loud."

Leaning down, he presses a kiss to my lips and leans back to smile. "I would have preferred that too."

And just when I think I couldn't be happier than at this very moment, he presses his forehead to mine and whispers, "What do you say we go to my place right now and wait for the stars to come out?"

I close my eyes and smile as I tell him I'd love to. When he takes me into his arms and holds me like I'm the most important thing in the world to him, I want to believe some quiet creature like me can be enough for the man who stood up on that bar and looked like a god to all those people and liked it. Because as much as he says he hates bartending and that's not what he usually does at his job, I saw how natural showing off was for him last night.

Will quiet nights and staring up at the stars be enough for Cade?

CHAPTER FOUR

ailey

His apartment looks the same as it did the last
time I was here, but something feels different. I can't
put my finger on exactly what that could be, though.
My eyes scan the living room for something new.
Nothing. It looks just like it did that night I was here.

Same neutral colored walls. Same black sectional.
Same end tables.

"Did you change something since I was here last?"
I ask as he heads for the kitchen.

Cade looks back and shakes his head. "No. I
haven't touched a thing since the designer came in and
did her thing. That was over a year ago."

I follow him into the kitchen and glance around in
this room. It looks the same, but I can't shake the
nagging feeling something's different in his place.

"I'm parched. What do you want to drink?" he asks from behind the refrigerator door.

"Whatever you have," I answer absentmindedly, still searching for what's changed here.

He pops his head up from behind the door and holds up a container of water and a jug of lemonade. "Either one of these work? I have some beer if you're feeling like drinking."

"Lemonade might be good. I had water all day."

We sound like two people who've been together for forty years. When did that happen? And why can't I figure out what's different about his apartment?

Then it comes to me. Nothing's changed here. Not the furniture or the décor or even Cade. They're all the same as the last time we were here together.

I'm the one that's changed. What happened last night has made me feel like I need to be on the lookout for anything different here.

I hate that. I don't want to constantly be thinking he's doing something behind my back so I need to inspect every square inch of this place every time I come here. That's not who I am or who I want to be.

Cade hands me a glass of lemonade and clinks my glass with his glass of water. "You were quiet all the way over here, so here's to us talking more. Actually, just you talking more. I've talked more today than I think I have in the entire last year."

I take a sip of the sweet drink with a hint of tartness that hits my tongue like the taste of lemonade always does and set my glass down on the counter.

"I'm trying really hard not to be scared right now. I hope that doesn't sound ridiculous."

God, that makes me sound so vulnerable. I didn't mean to say it like that.

But he doesn't seem bothered by what I said at all and walks over to stand in front of me. Smiling, he brushes my hair away from my face and kisses me softly on the lips. "It doesn't sound ridiculous. I fucked up, so it's only natural you'd be a little gun-shy. But you don't have to be. There's absolutely nothing between us that isn't true. I even told you some stuff that I never wanted you to know, so there's nothing to hide here."

His brown eyes look so sincere that I hate I even let myself think like I did when I walked into this place. He did tell me some pretty real stuff back at the restaurant, but I liked hearing all of it.

"You can tell me anything, Cade. Honest. I won't hold your past against you. All I care about is how you are while we're together. That's why last night bothered me so much, but you said your piece and I believe you, so today is a fresh start."

"Good. I want you to know something else, though."

When he doesn't continue, my stomach does a flip and butterflies fill me. I wait for him to continue, but he doesn't. Instead, he simply stares down into my eyes, which only makes me sure he's about to tell me something upsetting.

"If it's bad, you don't have to. It's okay."

He slides his arms around my waist and in a low

voice says, "I feel like you're trying to run away right now. Are you?"

Looking away, I nod. "When you didn't say what you said you wanted to, I got a little freaked out." I stop and take a deep breath before turning my head to face him. "But I'm not going anywhere physically, so I'm making progress. Don't you think?"

With a sweet smile, he sighs. "I do. But I must be getting better at picking up on it because it felt like you were a million miles away and I wanted to make sure you stayed, so I wrapped my arms around you. You don't have to run from me, Hailey. I promise I won't fuck up again."

I touch my palms to his chest, feeling the muscles underneath his shirt and wishing I could touch his body beneath the fabric. "So what did you want to tell me?"

He takes my right hand and places it over his heart. "I wanted you to know that I missed you. I know it was only one night, really, but I couldn't stop thinking that I'd never get to be like this with you again. Every time I thought that, it felt like someone was pressing down on my chest right where your hand is."

His skin feels warm against mine, like he's so much more alive than I am. I don't know if it's because he's fearless and not afraid of being hurt or if this is just who he is, but his ability to confess something like that leaves me in awe.

"I missed you too. I was sure I'd never be here with you again, and that made me sad."

"Well, no more sadness. No more missing either. The past is gone, and now we get to spend tonight together. Any ideas of what we should do?"

The way his eyes sparkle practically telegraphs what he's thinking. The feel of his hard cock pressing against my hip gives me an even bigger clue.

"Not that I can read minds or anything, but I think I know what you want to do," I say and giggle as I angle my hip toward the front of his pants.

Worry fills his eyes, and he shakes his head. "I don't want you to think that's all I want to do. I get that I fucked up. If that means we don't sleep together tonight, that's fine. My cock thinks other things, though, but you don't have to listen to him. He has a mind of his own, pretty much."

Cradling his face, I kiss him long and deep, sliding my tongue into his mouth to taste him like I've wanted to for so long today. When I lean back and smile, he looks relieved, like he didn't expect me to let him back in so quickly.

"I'm not the type of person to punish you for something you've said you're sorry for, Cade. I accepted your apology, so not sleeping with you tonight would be petty."

I slide my hand along the hard ridge in his pants and smile up at him. "Plus, punishing you punishes me, and I definitely don't think I deserve to be punished like that."

"You very well might be the perfect woman. Most women I've known love to punish guys that way," he says before letting out a low moan while I continue to rub him through his pants.

"Not perfect. It's just the way I am."

He nuzzles my neck, making me want so much more than just talking here in his kitchen. "Well, I like the way you are. The more I find out about you, the more I like, in fact."

My fingers slowly comb through his soft hair as he plants kisses just under my ear. I'd have to be insane to not want to sleep with Cade tonight or any night. Assuming he lives up to his promises. No woman in her right mind would deny herself what he has to offer after he's apologized.

I might be afraid of a million things in life and still working out my problems with my doctor, but I'm no fool. It's not every day a gorgeous man like Cade March walks into your life. Only a woman who doesn't enjoy feeling good would say no to sex with him tonight.

HE WRAPS HIS ARMS AROUND ME FROM BEHIND, AND as much as I want us to be in that bed together fucking because he's got me so excited, I love how safe and protected he makes me feel when he holds me like this. I lean my head back against his chest and cover his hands on my stomach with mine.

"I could stay like this all night," he whispers in my ear.

"That would make sex difficult since we're both dressed," I say with a giggle.

His hands slide up my body to cup my breasts while he nudges his cock against my lower back. "I like the way you have no problem wanting sex. That's pretty cool. No games or using it as a punishment. I like that."

Turning in his arms, I slide my hands under his black T-shirt to feel his soft, warm skin against my palms. "I'm a hundred other problems, I admit, but when it comes to sex, I'm not ashamed to say I like it. I particularly like it with you."

"Oh yeah? Why's that?"

I drag my fingernails along the space between his hipbones and feel his skin flutter from my touch. "Fishing for compliments? Okay, I like giving them when someone deserves it. The last time we were together, I thought I might pass out when I came. That's how good you are, so not being with you tonight was never not going to happen. I mean, once you came to see me and apologized. From that moment, it was game on."

His eyes grow wide as I tell him the truth, and when I finish, he shakes his head and smiles. "Damn. I didn't think you could get sexier, but that's fucking hot. Did you really almost pass out?"

I sense this isn't fishing but true disbelief, so I nod and shrug. "Yeah. It was good. Or maybe I just have low blood pressure."

Cade slides his tongue seductively along his lower lip. "I'm going with option one. It was that damn good."

"Well, you should because I've never had any

blood pressure issues high or low. I think you might just be a great lay."

Again, his eyes get wide, but this time I think he's really shocked at how I describe him. No point in lying. Cade March is incredible in bed.

"I don't know if I'm taking that as a compliment or just blown away that a woman said that to me that way. Either one works."

With my fingernail, I trace the outline of his very erect cock through his pants and smile up at him. "I'm having a hard time believing no woman has ever said that to you before."

He tilts his head back and moans when I circle the tip of it a few times. "Not that I can remember, but maybe it's just the way you phrased it. God, I don't know what you're doing with your fingernail right now, but it feels fucking fantastic."

"Better than what I can do with my tongue?" I tease.

Cade looks down at me and scowls. "No way. That's a hundred times better."

"Then maybe we should do that," I say with a smile as I unzip his pants.

His gaze stays fixed on my face while I lower myself to the floor. Kneeling in front of him, I tug his cock out of his pants and bite my lip at how sexy he looks staring down at me in anticipation of the first moment my tongue will touch him.

For a few seconds, I close my eyes and inhale a deep breath to take his scent in. He's all male, muskiness mixed with the clean scent of soap that makes me want him even more.

With a gentle grip, I guide his cock to my mouth. Just as I part my lips, I open my eyes and look up at Cade to see him watching me with rapt fascination. His intense gaze tells me he's dying to feel my mouth on him, and a second later, I give him what he wants.

What we both want.

A hint of saltiness hits my taste buds when he glides over my tongue toward the back of my throat as I take as much of him into me as I can. Long and thick, he's blessed with a great cock, but I'm not blessed with the skills to deep throat, so I only get a little over half of him into my mouth before I have to back off.

"Jesus, that feels so fucking good," he groans above me, making my inability to do what I really wish I could do a little less disappointing.

His hands burrow into my hair, tugging me back down onto him faster this time. Afraid he might slam into the back of my throat so I gag, I keep my hand at the base of his cock, tightening it with every inch I go lower.

We fall into a rhythm that I like and he loves, if his moans above me are any clue. I flick my tongue along the underside of him, over the vein that runs the full length of his cock, and each time, he tightens his fists in my hair a little more so licks of pain skitter across my scalp.

"Fuck, Hailey…don't stop. That feels incredible,"

he whispers breathlessly, and I look up to see his eyes closed now.

I sense he's not far from coming, so I speed up just a little and begin to move my hand to stroke his cock in time with my mouth sucking him. With my left hand, I drag my fingernails across his skin between his hips, and he reacts immediately with another sultry moan that sounds like it comes from deep inside him.

He's sensual and erotic standing above me, and I can't get enough of how it feels to please him. His happiness makes me happy. His pleasure gives me pleasure.

All of a sudden, his hands leave my hair and I see him look down at me, his eyes big like he's scared of something. Before he can say anything, the first taste of cum hits my tongue and I moan against his cock, closing my eyes as I continue to take every inch of him I can.

When he finishes, I sit back on my heels and tilt my head to look up at him. He looks flushed and satisfied. If it's possible, he's even better looking than ever before.

"I took my hands away and hoped you knew that was me trying to say I was about to come. I guess we got our signals crossed?" he asks quietly.

God, he can be cute.

Shaking my head, I smile. "I had a feeling that's what you meant, but I didn't need a signal. I knew you were almost there."

"So you're not angry I came in your mouth?" he asks innocently.

"No. I guess I could have had you come on my chest, but since I'm still dressed, that would make a mess. Did you want to come somewhere else?"

I know the answer to that, but he's too cute about all of this so I can't resist teasing him a little. A look of recognition comes over him a few seconds later, and he pulls me up to kiss him.

"You are officially the sexiest woman I've ever known. Hands down."

"Because I had you come in my mouth? That seems like a pretty low bar since you went down on me and finished."

His dark eyes dance as he looks down at me and shakes his head. "Seriously, the sexiest woman. You have no idea what it means that you aren't pissed. I was bracing for some real anger there."

"That sounds like a mood killer. What kind of women have you been with before me?"

"All the wrong ones," he says sweetly before kissing me again. "Definitely all the wrong ones."

CHAPTER FIVE

ade

I ROLL ONTO MY BACK, MY SKIN COVERED IN SWEAT and my body aching in places I didn't realize I had muscles. Hailey lies next to me, her head on the pillow and her hair spread out behind her so she looks like a mermaid.

An unbelievably sexy mermaid who may have just fucked me into oblivion.

"So, I'm not sure how to phrase this, so I'm going to go with what's in my head and hope you don't get upset. Were you a call girl in a prior life or something?"

She laughs and rolls her eyes, instantly putting me at ease because I suspected she might throw a punch for a question like that. "Why do men always assume you can only learn to be good in bed if you do it a lot? Haven't you guys ever heard of reading?"

"So you read how-to books on sex? Whatever they are, you clearly got what they were teaching."

Hailey inches over and kisses me. "No, but I read romance books. They were a few of the things that got me through when I didn't want to go on all those months. There are some pretty graphic ones, and I just mimicked what I read."

"Really?"

Is it possible this woman is that incredible that she learned how to be fucking fantastic in bed from reading? What are these books with such magic in them?

"Yeah," she says like it's just the normal kind of thing everyone does. "It's how I learned to bake, and it's how I learned to fuck."

I wrap my arm around her and pull her to me, loving the feel of her next to my body. "I think you might be the most amazing person I've ever met."

"I bet you'd find lots of women read romance novels and learn some skills from them. I don't think it's anything amazing," she says nonchalantly as she curls up against my side.

"Well, I love it."

And then, as if the words have a mind of their own and I can't stop them, I say the three words I've never uttered to a woman. "I love you."

They sound strange coming out of my mouth, and for a long moment they hang in the air around us, neither one of us saying a word to break the silence.

My heartbeat pounds in my ears when I realize what I just said for the first time in my life.

I told someone I love them. And as odd as that is, it feels worse since she isn't saying it back to me.

Hailey lifts her head off my chest and looks at me strangely, like she isn't sure she heard correctly. "Did you just say you love me?"

Now seems like as good a time as any for some humor, so I shake my head. "Nah. I wouldn't say that. I mean, I could since I know those three words, but that would be crazy. Right?"

"Well, okay. I was going to say I love you too, but since you didn't say that, I won't say that either. Glad we got that straightened out."

She moves to set her head down on my chest again, but I roll her over onto her back and kiss her. "So if I did say it, you wouldn't run from the room in terror?"

Those beautiful blue eyes stare up at me with such sweetness in them as she shakes her head and smiles. "No. No running. I'd stay right here, and I might even say them back."

"Should we try a second take and see what happens?"

Hailey lifts her head off the pillow and kisses me. "Let's try."

As much as I always thought saying those three words would be the scariest thing I could ever utter, they come out like they're the most natural thing I could say to her at this moment. "I love you, Hailey."

She doesn't miss a beat before she says the words that sound like music to my ears. "I love you, Cade."

"I've never said that in my life."

"You did a good job. All the words came out in the right order and very clear. I understood every one of them," she says with a giggle.

"I don't know why they came out, but I'm glad they did."

"I'm glad they did too because I feel that way. I know it's probably crazy because we haven't been seeing each other for very long at all, but I have said those words before and I know I felt a little like this when I did."

Jealousy races through me at hearing her say she's told someone before me she loved them. Not that I should be surprised since she was engaged to that jackass who cheated on her. Of course, she said it to him.

I just never thought about how much I hate that idea until this very moment.

"Oh, yeah. I guess you would have. So this time felt like that time?"

Hailey shakes her head and wraps her arms around my body to pull me close. "Sort of, but not exactly. It took six months for us to say it to one another. I guess that should have been a clue, huh?"

"So a little over two weeks and after one major fuck up seems fast, I guess."

"It seems right, Cade. And to celebrate it, I think we should have sex again. There's this thing I want to try that involves me on top and my legs out to the side.

45

I have an idea in my head about it, but I'd like to see if it will work. You up for it?"

I roll my hips so she can feel I'm ready to go again. "You're not just trying to distract me from thinking about you and that guy saying you love each other are you? Because I'm fine if you are. I'm not going to turn down sex with you, so if that's what you're doing, I'm all in."

She wraps her legs around my waist and presses her pussy against my cock. "You don't have to worry about him. He found someone else before he even left me, so there's nothing there. I'm really a one-man kind of woman, so since I already said I loved you, I guess you're that man."

Looking down into her soft eyes, I feel my jealousy ebb away. "You must think I'm crazy to be jealous of someone I've never met."

Hailey trails her fingertips down over my chest and stomach. "I was jealous of a woman I only saw from twenty feet away and never spoke to, so I don't think it's that crazy."

I can't let her think for even a second Kylie meant anything with that dance of hers, so I tilt Hailey's chin up and press a kiss to her lips. "I know why you were, but you had no reason to be jealous."

"Promise?"

Her eyes fill with so much hope and anticipation that I can't let her down now. But honestly, I'd promise her the moon at this moment, so promising there's no reason to be jealous of any other woman on the planet is the easiest thing in the world to do.

"I promise. It's all you, Hailey."

"Okay."

"So we should probably get to having sex again because any more talk and both of us are going to get out of the mood."

That gets me an adorable smile. "I think we both know that's not going to happen."

She's the perfect woman. That seals it.

CLUB X DURING THE DAY ALWAYS REMINDS ME OF what I see when I first wake up in the morning after having a wild party at my house the night before. Even if I cleaned up before crashing, my place looks too stark, too bright when I wake up.

Normally, that's because I'm so hungover I can't handle the sunlight trying to find its way into my room. But the club looks like that every time I come here during the daytime.

Stark and brutal.

At night, it's all fun and games. The colored lights break up the pitch black but just enough to make everyone look like a far more interesting version of themselves. The music adds to the fun, so people appear like in some kind of wild dream.

If they walked in here right now, I wouldn't recognize them. They wouldn't recognize me either. That's the beauty of night and the terrible reality of day for you.

The club stands empty, like a hollow cavern devoid

of all its good times. No one's here since it's only early afternoon, but in the office, I hear a noise that sounds like someone talking on the phone.

I push the door open and see my father with his feet up on the desk and his cell phone to his ear. This is the image I have of him from my earliest memories as a child. My mother used to bring me here to see him and the three of us would eat lunch together in this office with no windows and only that one door.

Even as a three year old kid, I always felt trapped as soon as I walked in, but my father loved this part of the club. Everyone else thinks the fun is out there on the dance floor and at the bar, but for Stefan March, the truly good stuff happens right here where he makes his plans and runs the entire show from that desk he's had all my life.

When he sees me walk in, his eyes get wide and he waves me over, like he's eager to talk to me. He probably wants to rave about that damn anniversary party again.

"Let me talk to you later, Dan. My son just walked in, so I want to see what he's up to," he says, again waving me over to sit down.

Smiling, he nods at whatever the guy on the phone is talking about and says, "Got it! Sounds good. Okay, let's catch up with each other later in the week and see what's going on. Talk to you later, Dan."

A second later, he tosses the cell phone onto his desk and leans back in his chair as he runs his hand through his hair. "There's no way in hell I'm working with that son of a bitch again. I don't care how much he thinks he can sweet talk me."

I give him a half-hearted smile since I have no idea who this son of a bitch is or what he did in the past to make him persona non grata with my father. He probably cheated him on something. That's a surefire way to get on his bad side.

"So what brings you down here in the middle of the day? I can't remember the last time you saw this place when the sun was out."

Probably when he had me running the club and I had to deal with all those goddamned vendors and the million and a half problems that come with them. I don't say that, though, since I don't want to get into a conversation about that again.

"I need to talk to you about something, Dad. Before I get into this, I want you to know this is non-negotiable. If you can't agree to this, then I can't work here anymore. I don't think I'm being unreasonable, but if you do, then I guess we'll be at an impasse."

When I finish speaking, he nods and gives me a big smile. "Sounds pretty serious. Only one problem."

"What's that?" I ask, already fucking defensive.

"You haven't even told me what you're here about and already you've got me unwilling to agree with you. At least give me a chance to be a hard ass, Cade."

Damn. I'd been so convinced he'd say no immediately, I never even got to what I won't be doing anymore if I keep working here.

"Oh, yeah. Well, I guess that would help," I admit, feeling pretty foolish.

My father chuckles and puts his hands back behind his head, clearly enjoying this more than I am. "You never know. I might disappoint you this time and think you're right. It has happened before, you know."

"Not often," I mumble.

"Well, how about we try to make it happen more often? You're not a boy anymore, and as your mother reminds me more often than I like, you have your own life to lead. So tell me what's on your mind and we can take it from there."

So be it. He wants to know what I'm thinking? Now he will.

"If I'm going to be bartending here anymore, I'm not going to do any more of that bullshit that Kylie pulled the other night. I nearly lost someone I care about because of that. So no more."

He shrugs and gives me a nod. "Okay. No more. We talked about this the other night, though. Didn't we?"

"The other night I was out of my mind angry. Today, I'm thinking straight. I won't do that again and risk Hailey finding out. She wouldn't understand."

My mention of her name makes him lean forward. "So your girlfriend's name is Hailey. Is this the infamous young woman who my brothers and Alex can't say enough about with the desserts? Is that the same Hailey?"

I cringe at the thought that my family has already begun to discuss my girlfriend. Nothing good can come from that.

"Yes, and I never realized all the men in the family

were such gossips. Maybe you guys could talk about something else. We have sports teams in this city I know you guys are fans of. You could talk about them. Or a million other topics. You've known each other all your lives, right?"

My father smiles, but remains silent for a long moment. Folding his arms across his chest, he finally says, "You're a little touchy about this subject, Cade. I'm not saying we were all sitting around talking about this woman. Your uncles and cousin were actually very impressed with her talent at making desserts. That's all. Nobody's gossiping about her."

I need to change the subject now before we go down this rabbit hole and he starts pumping me for information I don't want to give any of them just yet. Better to focus on my reason for being here.

"Whatever. The point is I'm not interested in being a show pony anymore. I'll tend bar. That's it. If that means you have to put me at the back bar or upstairs, that's fine. I'm not doing this for money anyway."

He surprises me when he nods again. "Okay, that works for me. But I'm a little confused. The other night, you didn't act like Hailey was anyone important. How was I to know what Kylie was doing would be a problem? You wouldn't even refer to Hailey as your girlfriend, if I remember correctly."

As much as I hate to admit it, he is remembering correctly. That was then, though. This is now, and now she's my girlfriend.

"That's true, but things have changed."

To me, this conversation is over, so I move to leave,

happy to have gotten all I wanted out of our little talk. But as I stand up, my father asks the question I always dread about anyone I'm seeing.

"Will we get to meet this girlfriend any time soon?"

I wince at the very words when they hit my ears. Nothing would make him and my mother happier than my bringing a girlfriend to meet them, have dinner, and hang out for a few hours. And nothing makes my stomach twist into knots more.

"We'll see, Dad."

On my way to the door, he adds, "Because I know your mother would be over the moon to finally meet one of your girlfriends. She never gets a chance, but she'd be thrilled to, Cade."

The doubt in his voice tells me he doesn't think it will ever happen. Good. Maybe he won't mention it to my mother and I won't have to deal with having to put her off about this topic yet again like I have countless times.

"Well, then don't tell her about it and she won't get her hopes up. We've only been dating for two weeks, so it's a little early for all this talk anyway."

I hear him chuckle behind me and turn around to see him grinning at me. "Something funny?"

"Just that I thought this was farther along than it is. Two weeks is nothing in Cade time. I thought this was something more involved."

The smug look on his face bothers me, and even though I know I shouldn't let him bait me like he always does, I walk back toward him and ask, "What the hell is Cade time?"

My father shrugs. "Just the way we think of how long you generally are with your girlfriends. Here today, gone tomorrow. Two weeks is nothing. When it gets to be a couple months, then it will be something."

"It's something now," I snap, barely able to contain the anger rising in me.

"Sure, sure, but you're famous for going through women like a fish goes through water, Cade. You can't expect your mother to get excited about every girl you see. She'd be finding out about a new one every few days."

I shouldn't say anything to that, but I can't stop myself. "It's like you don't remember being my age, Dad. Like having a good time is a problem. But for your information, I'm not just having a good time with Hailey. Not that I plan on bringing her around any of you guys in our fine family since it's clear everyone thinks I'm nothing but a guy who goes through women like I change my underwear. I can imagine the word manwhore being thrown around."

Damnit, I hate that every time my father and I talk for more than two goddamned minutes it ends up like this. I don't know if it's because we're too alike or too different. Whatever it is that makes us like this, it's fucking exhausting.

Before he can keep this thing between us going, I turn around and head for the door. "See you later, Dad. Tell Mom I'll call her."

"Call your sister too, Cade. Ava thinks you've fallen off the face of the earth."

"Got it. Call all the women. Bye!"

CHAPTER SIX

*H*ailey

EVERYONE FROM HECTOR TO MY MOTHER HAS BEEN giving me strange looks since I got to the restaurant this morning. I can't tell if they're worried about me or if they can't figure out why I'm happy. I catch them looking over at me while they're working and then when I meet their gazes, they quickly turn away all sheepishly.

"Honey, the apple tarts are all gone already. Did you make more?" my mother asks in her usual way, but I sense she's looking for a way to start a conversation.

About what, I don't know. Well, that's not true. I think she might want to ask about what happened with Cade because I haven't said a word about it since I walked in this morning.

I grab the tray of tarts behind me and hand them to her. "All set and ready to go!"

She doesn't walk away, so after a few seconds, I can't avoid glancing up at her. She's giving me that look of anticipation, like she's hoping this is the time when she'll find her in and be able to ask me all about what happened yesterday.

"You okay, Mom? Anything wrong with the tarts?" I ask, barely able to keep the smile from my face as she squirms trying to think of a way to ask me the question she's been dying to for hours.

Nodding, she gives me a smirk as her dark blond hair falls into her eyes. She looks around for somewhere to set the tray down so she can push it off her face, so I reach out to take it from her.

"Here, I got that for you. You seem flustered today, Mom. Everything all right?"

When she finishes fixing her hair, she reaches out for the tray again, still looking like she wants to talk but doesn't know how to start the conversation. "I'm fine. How are you?"

There's her in.

"I'm good. Really good. You sure you're okay? Because it feels like you might want to talk about something, but you don't seem to say much every time you come back to my area here."

Now I can't stop myself from smiling. Teasing her is too much fun.

"Stop playing with me, Hailey Marie Canton. You know what I want to talk about. You've known all day while you let me twist in the wind trying to find a way to ask," she says, giving me her best angry Mom grimace complete with furious pursed lips and frustrated pulled in eyebrows that nearly meet in the center of her nose.

"Why didn't you just ask then?"

Her frown deepens, if that's possible. "Your father said I should let you bring it up. That's what I get for listening to his suggestions. Do you know he wanted to make tuna fish and have it as a Tuesday special? 'Tuna for Tuesday,' he said. Just crazy."

I listen to her go off on my father for a little bit and finally she stops to take a breath. "Don't the tarts need to go out to the case?" I ask.

"No. Well, yes, but they can wait."

"Okay. So what did you want to ask me then?"

Her frustration practically boils over, and she huffs, "Well, what happened with Cade, of course? You were upset yesterday and then you left with him and we didn't see you until you showed up here for work this morning. Did you two make up?"

Now my smile reflects my genuine happiness in being able to say we did. "Yes. He explained things, and I accepted his apology."

For the first time today, she smiles, and it seems like all the stress drains from her body right in front of me. "Oh, that's good! I know you like spending time with him, honey. As long as you're happy, I'm happy. I think your father likes him too. He seemed genuinely pleased that Cade came over and you two were talking yesterday."

A laugh escapes from my throat after how he acted

yesterday. "He gave him the angry dad face. I think he thought he was helping."

"Oh, that's your father's way of being a dad. He did that with your sisters too. Danielle used to tell him not to do it all the time. I swear every boyfriend she had got that look," she says, waving away the concern she thinks I have about my father trying to act all tough for me.

"He didn't have to, Mom. Cade's a good guy. It was just a misunderstanding. Everything's fine now."

"Good. I'm glad. Well, I better get these tarts out front," she says before hurrying off.

Calling after her, I say, "Be sure to tell Dad what we talked about. I'm sure he's dying to know."

From across the kitchen, Hector says, "That's all he could talk about yesterday. We all were worried about you."

He gives me a wink like he does whenever he says something sweet, and I smile back. I'm not a fan of having my private life spread all over the restaurant, but I know my father meant no harm. I know Hector and the rest of the cooks are just curious. How could they not be when my father probably spent the entire night talking about how worried he was?

They saw me at my worst when I first came back here to work a year ago. Then my parents watched over me like a baby bird, worried that at any minute I might give up on everything. To the people in the kitchen, I think I started out as some oddity and gradually became someone they cared about. It's only natural that they're interested in my life now that something's actually happening in it.

My mother rushes into the kitchen, her arms waving in front of her like something's on fire. I jump up from my chair as she runs up to me, unsure what could be wrong.

"Mom, what's happened?"

Her eyes wide and flashing with excitement, she says, "That food blogger who was on the morning show the other day is out talking to your father about your tarts! She's raving about them, Hailey!"

"Who? What morning show? The local one or the national one? What's her name, Mom?" I ask as my heart races in anticipation of my hearing who this woman is who loves my apple tarts so much.

"Brooke Dunning!" my mother answers, saying her name like I should know her.

"I don't know who that is, Mom."

"She's huge! I saw her on the local morning show, but they said she's a food blogger who's known around the world. You should go out to talk to her. She's just as nice as can be, and she's got the cutest hair. Go out and see."

I hurry to pull my apron over my head and brush myself off since I'm covered in flour from making the tarts. Oh, God! Why did I have to make such a simple dessert today? Apple tarts are so basic. Any fool with some flour and apples can make them. Why didn't I try the macarons I wanted to? They would have been so much better.

My mother tugs my arm to get me to move. "What

are you waiting for, Hailey? Get out there and talk to her. I promise you she's very nice. Not conceited or pretentious at all like some of those foodies have been."

It suddenly dawns on me that Brooke Dunning, famous food blogger, is talking to my father, a man who sees no use for what she does and has nothing but disdain for people like her. At this very moment, he's probably lecturing her on why food blogger posts shouldn't include all that information about them and should focus on the restaurant, the chef, and the food, most of all. If I don't get out there right now, he'll likely chase her away with his bad attitude about what she's chosen to do with her life.

I rush toward the kitchen doors and suddenly stop to spin around to face my mother. "Do I look okay? Is there anything on my face that shouldn't be there?"

She gives me one of those wonderful smiles that have always made everything okay. "You look beautiful, honey. Now go out there and impress her."

One deep breath in and out and I walk through the doors to find my father giving his talk on how important the restaurant is compared to any story about the food. I cringe at how long it took me to get out here and hurry over, hoping to stop him before he says something really insulting.

"Hi! Dad, I'm sure Brooke isn't interested in all this talk about how you'd write about food."

My father takes the hint, thankfully, and excuses himself so Brooke and I are left alone. Beautiful, with short black hair and stunning green eyes that remind me of a cat's, she's tall and willowy like a model. I'm instantly impressed and intimidated, all at the same time.

"Hailey, it's so nice to meet you. You are all anyone can talk about in this town when it comes to food, so I knew I had to make my way down here to Comfort Food to meet you and try one of your delectable desserts. I am absolutely in love with this apple tart! I've never had anything so light and yet so sweet in my life."

As she talks, she touches my forearms and I notice she has very long nails and they're painted in a French manicure. I can't imagine how she makes any dish with those things at the end of her fingers.

"It's so great to meet you too," I say, not as gushing as her but still very polite. "And thank you for saying such kind things about the tarts. I wish I knew you were coming today. I would have made something far more elaborate and special."

She waves her right hand through the air between us, those long nails flying past my nose. "No need. The most special food in the world is the kind that makes people feel good. That's what I always say. And those tarts of yours made me feel out of this world. I'll have to do three extra spin classes just to work off all those calories, but it was so worth it."

My gaze instinctively drops for a moment at her mention of calories, and I glance down at her flat stomach and tiny waist highlighted by the black belt on her red dress. Three extra spin classes might make her so thin she'll slip under the door.

I quickly look up and smile. "I'm so happy you enjoyed them. They're one of my favorite desserts to make."

For a second time, she waves her hand in the air in front of me, but this time the left hand joins in. I gently lean back just an inch or so and give her a bigger smile as I hope she doesn't notice how uneasy those nails of hers make me.

"So let me get to the point of my visit. I want you to join me on my podcast. You're on the lips of every food blogger in this area, so while I'm here, I want to make sure I get you on with me. Now you should know I never take no for an answer—it's the secret to my success—so don't even think of saying anything but yes."

All I can think of at this moment is that single word she insists I say. Of course, I'd agree to do her podcast. I'd be crazy not to jump at this chance.

"I'd love to," I say as calmly as I can, struggling to keep my voice from quivering.

Brooke's eyes get wide, and she waves her hands yet again in between us. "Oh, that's fantastic! Now usually you can do a podcast from your house or anywhere for that matter, but since I'm in town and we can be together, I'd love for you to come to my hotel next Friday. We'll talk food, you can tell my listeners all about your favorites, and everyone will love it. Feel free to bring whatever desserts you want. I'll block off time for those extra spin classes on my calendar today because I'm going to try every one of the delectable treats you bring."

"Next Friday it is, then," I say as my mind races to figure out what I can find to make in the next eight days that will bowl her over and impress whoever might be listening to her podcast.

She hands me her business card and flips it over in my hand. "My number is on there, so call me the day before and I'll tell you my hotel and room number. My publicist has me in one I'm not crazy about at the moment, so I'm thinking that's got to change. It doesn't even have a restaurant inside! Can you believe that? Who would ever think to put me in a hotel without a restaurant?"

I don't get the chance to say a word in response before she wraps her arms around my shoulders and brings me in for a big, unexpected hug. "Next Friday. I can't wait. See you then!"

"See you then."

Rushing away toward the door, she stops right before she reaches it and turns around looking almost guilty. "Any chance I can get another one of those apple tarts? I simply love them!"

"Of course! Let me grab you one," I say before hurrying over to the case and picking out two of the best looking tarts.

When I hand her the bag, she beams a smile and leans in to whisper in my ear, "This is going to mean four more spin classes, but it will be so worth it."

And then she walks away out the door, my apple tarts with her, and jumps into a black car before leaving as I stand there in the middle of my parents' little restaurant in shock at what's just happened. I don't get long to let it sink in before my mother and father rush out from the kitchen to ask me a million questions.

"We were watching through the window. She seemed so nice, Hailey. Did she take more tarts with her when she left?" my mother asks, practically breathless with excitement.

"She did. I gave her two more, and she had already had one with Daddy before I came out."

My father nods like he approves of all he's seen today. "She seemed very interested in your desserts. I think she must eat a lot of sugar to be that enthusiastic."

That gets my father a disapproving slap on the arm from my mother. "Robert! She was enthusiastic because of our daughter's fantastic apple tarts."

I don't bother adding that I think Brooke Dunning might be naturally hyper with a healthy dose of caffeine and sugar mixed in. Four spin classes to work off two apple tarts does seem like a bit much.

"She wants me to appear on her podcast next Friday. We're going to do it in her hotel. She said I should bring some of my desserts. What should I make? Maybe I could perfect the macarons before then, but they aren't elaborate or anything. Then again, she did say that food doesn't have to be elaborate. It just has to make someone feel good, and they would do the trick there. No, she said that about special food. Maybe. I don't know. It all happened so fast."

I don't know why, but now I feel like waving my

hands around like Brooke did. I don't have beautiful nails like hers, so I wouldn't be putting anyone in danger of losing an eye either.

My mother wraps her arms around me in a hug I sense is probably her way of trying to calm me down. Ever since I fell apart last year, if she thinks I'm unraveling even the slightest bit, she likes to hold me. It does help, but I'm not freaking out right now.

I'm just happy.

"It's okay, Mom. I'm good. Just excited. So many good things are happening right now."

Leaning back, she smiles at me before kissing my cheek. "All things you absolutely deserve."

"So what are you going to do now? You can't sit in that kitchen all day after having that kind of thing happen," my father says with a chuckle. "Seems like the kind of thing a young woman would want to tell a certain guy."

I feel my cheeks heat up at his thinly veiled mention of Cade. "I will. First, though, I have to tell Meadow. She's been predicting something big would happen ever since that first food blogger came in here and wrote about my desserts."

"Okay, honey. It's only right you remember the people who were there with you when you were nobody just starting out," he says, teasing me. "You will remember us little people when you hit the big time, won't you?"

Rolling my eyes, I give his arm a gentle nudge with my elbow. "Funny, Dad."

"Congratulations, honey. I'm so proud of you."

I give him a kiss on the cheek and head back to the kitchen to call Meadow. Ten minutes and nearly a dozen shrieks of excitement later, she makes me promise to tell her everything that happens with Brooke Dunning.

"It won't be as exciting as what you told me about Cade, but I'm here for any and all good news with you, Hailey. Promise me we'll go out to celebrate after you do her podcast. We have a lot to celebrate lately."

"I promise. I just hope I don't mess it all up. I've never done a podcast. What if I freeze and can't remember what to talk about?"

With a laugh, she says, "From what you told me about that Brooke woman, you will have to fight to get a word in edgewise. Don't worry. You're going to be great."

"Thanks, Meadow. I'll let you know how it goes as soon as I get done at her hotel room." I start to say goodbye, but then I remember she hasn't said anything about Alex yet.

"Hey, did you ever get to meet up with Alex that night we went to Club X? I feel bad about the fact that you had to rush me out of there and didn't get to even see him."

She lets out a sigh of frustration. "We've tried a few times, but our schedules aren't helping any. I'm not giving up on getting together with him yet, though," she says with her usual determination. "That man is way too hot to let work get in the way. But I have to go now. I want all the details on the food lady's podcast and your adventures with her as soon as it happens, so don't forget."

"I won't. Thanks, Meadow."

"You deserve it, Hailey. The podcast and how much fun you're having with Cade. Remember that."

As I call the man himself, I think about how hard it would have been to imagine so much good coming to me just six months ago. I don't know if I deserve it, like Meadow says, but I like it.

Actually, I love it.

CHAPTER SEVEN

ailey

AFTER NEARLY AN HOUR SITTING IN THE PASSENGER
seat of Cade's car wearing a blindfold, I think I might
be getting carsick. Between all the starts and stops and
his tendency to drive fast, my body doesn't know what
to do from one second to the next.

"Not to ruin whatever you're doing with this
surprise, but if I don't look out the window and get my
bearings, I think I might get sick."

Cade touches my hand resting on my leg and gives
my fingers a gentle squeeze. "I promise. Only a little
while more. I want you to be surprised. You asked me
to help you get away for a few days before your big
meeting, and that's exactly what we're doing."

I turn to face where I think he is and smile. "If I
could just lift this blindfold for a second, I think I

might be okay. I had no idea not being able to see where I'm going would do this to me."

"Just a couple minutes more. I promise."

The feel of his touch on my hand helps, but something about this blindfold and moving makes my stomach turn. Not exactly the way I wanted to start out this three-day vacation we're taking.

When I called Cade and told him about Brooke Dunning and her podcast, I began to unravel, just as my mother worried I would. Nothing too bad. Certainly nothing like what happened last year. But enough that I asked Cade if we could do something to take my mind off things for a couple days. I thought he'd suggest we hang out at his place, but he came up with the idea of going to a hotel and relaxing like a little mini-vacation.

How could I say no? It sounded perfect, and with him there with me, I knew it would be just what I need. So I whipped up a few batches of cherry turnovers, enough to last the time that I'll be gone, and told my parents I'd see them in a few days.

Now, however, I'm struggling not to throw up all over the inside of Cade's car because of this blindfold he insists I wear to keep where we're going a complete surprise.

"Okay, you can take it off. We're here!" he says with so much excitement in his voice that I practically rip the thing off my head.

I focus my eyes to see a sea green and white house with three floors looming in front of me. When we get out of the car, I see the house is even bigger up close.

Turning my head to the sound of a boat behind us, I see water as I look through the side yard. "Where are we? I thought you said we were going to a hotel for a few days."

Cade cups my elbow with his hand and guides me toward the house in front of me. "I was going to do that, but then I heard of somewhere even better. Welcome to the newest house owned by Alexandria March. I think she's thinking of calling it something like Cupid's Cove. When you meet her, you'll understand why that makes sense."

We walk through the front door and begin to climb the white painted steps toward the second floor. "Alexandria March? Is Alex named after her?"

Behind me, Cade laughs. "Yep. My mother and his mother, my aunt Olivia, were pregnant at the same time. Both of them were thinking of naming us Alexander after her, but they finally decided he would get that name, even though he was born three months after me. I got the consolation prize of having Alexander as my middle name, though."

I look back at him as we near the top of the steps and ask, "Is his middle name Cade then?"

He stops when we reach the second floor and thinks for a moment. "I don't think so, but I just realized now I don't think I know what Alex's middle name is. If his brother wasn't named after their father, I'd guess Cassian, but he is, so I don't know."

"Maybe Oliver after his mother?" I ask, half-joking.

Cade shrugs. "Maybe. So what do you think of the place?"

For the first time, I look at the home he's brought me to and nearly have trouble catching my breath. The pale blue painted room seems to go on forever, and there are windows everywhere so you can see out onto the water. It might be the prettiest room I've ever stood in.

"It's beautiful, Cade. This is your grandmother's home?"

He sets down our bags on a nearby table and shakes his head. "No. Just one she bought. She's all about real estate. She's pretty much the reason I bought my condo. When I first started getting my trust fund, she sat me down and told me all the reasons she thinks a home is the most important thing a person can own. I had no intentions of buying a condo before that, but she convinced me. I think this is her third home on the island here."

"Where are we? I don't think I've ever been to this island in my life."

Waving me over to him, he takes my hand and begins to walk toward the windows. "Anna Maria Island. She says it's her favorite place on earth."

"And she doesn't have a problem with the two of us spending the next few days here?" I ask as the image of an old woman coming at me with a rolling pin in her hand for sleeping in the same bed as her grandson flashes through my mind.

My question makes him throw his head back and laugh. "No way. My grandmother had to deal with three sons who were nothing but trouble when they were my age. She's the one who suggested we use this place until she figures out what she wants to do with it. She basically collects houses. She also likes to spoil all of her grandchildren rotten. So you don't have to worry."

As I look out onto the blue water below, I can't believe how beautiful this view is or that I'm standing here with Cade getting to enjoy it. "This is incredible. Thank you so much for bringing me here. I just wanted to relax for a couple days before I have to go do Brooke Dunning's podcast. I know it doesn't sound like much, but it made me get a little crazy there for a minute or two, and that's why I asked you to help me get away. I never expected anything like this, Cade. I would have been happy with a couple nights at your condo or even a motel on the side of the highway."

Nuzzling my neck, he moves behind me and wraps his arms around my shoulders. I love when he holds me like this every time we look out at the water off his balcony. Here it feels even better because he made this happen just for me.

"I don't think I've ever seen the Gulf look so good, you know that?" he says in a soft voice near my ear.

"I didn't even know that was the water I was looking at. I thought maybe it was some bay. You're so lucky to have this in your life. You really are. Your family must be really incredible to let you enjoy this."

He chuckles low in my ear before kissing my neck. "Some of them are, but what I'm lucky to have in my life is you."

The way he says that makes me feel so safe and loved. I missed this feeling all those months when I hid away and swore I'd never take a chance on another relationship and another guy again.

Covering his hands with mine, he tells me about how when he was a little boy, he and his cousins would come to this island and play on the beach building sandcastles and burying one another in the sand. The way he talks about growing up like that makes me hopeful I'll get to meet more of his family other than Alex. So far, if he's any indication of what the rest of the March clan is like, I can't see why I won't adore all of them.

"You sound like you had a great childhood," I say, looking back at him.

He thinks about that for a second and nods. "Some of it was really great. I didn't have any brothers, but I had Alex who was like a twin brother since we were born three months apart and my cousins were like brothers. I think if you said that to my sister she might have a different opinion since there are no other girls, though. Well, except for my uncle Kane and aunt Abbi's daughter, but she's older than the rest of us so by the time we were old enough to play together, she was in high school and couldn't be bothered with us."

"So your cousins are all close in age with you?"

Cade rests his chin on my shoulder as he explains, "Four boys born within three years' time. My family pretty much exploded in thirty-six months. Then my uncle Kane decided he wanted to adopt Wilder after all he'd been through, so by the time we all were teenagers, there were five of us. Trust me, we were the terrors of our high school. Be glad you didn't meet me or Alex back then. You'd never speak to either of us again."

The way he says that doesn't scare me off but intrigues me, so I turn my back on the beautiful scene of the Gulf late in the afternoon and look up at him. "I bet you guys were heartbreakers. Way too cute for your own good and way too cocky for everyone else's good."

Cade gives me a sexy smile that never fails to make me think he's even more gorgeous than he was the last time I looked at him. "Times the cockiness by ten. I'm not sure you'd call us heartbreakers, though. More like bumbling fools who thought they were way too slick for high school. Trust me, you shouldn't be surprised if we're out in public one day and some woman walks right up to me and slaps me across the face. I may not even remember her, but with the way we were, I probably have it coming in spades."

"Why would anyone do that?" I wonder aloud, sure this incredible guy who did all of this for me just because I asked couldn't deserve that kind of treatment.

For a moment, he bites his bottom lip like he isn't sure he wants to tell me just how bad he and his cousins were back then. "Well, let's just say the five of us had reputations for being less than wonderful guys at times and leave it at that."

The image of Cade being a bad boy doesn't really force me to stretch my mind much, but that doesn't bother me. Who he was before he met me, even if he was that person just days before, doesn't matter. It's who he is now I care about, and today, he's the man who brought me to this beautiful home overlooking the Gulf of Mexico to relax with him for the next few days.

I press my palms against his chest and stand on my tiptoes to kiss him. "Thankfully, no one holds who we were in high school against us."

With a wink, he says with a grin, "Except that woman who slaps me across the face one day. She's going to be holding a lot against me."

More relaxed than I've been in so long I can't remember, I rest my head on his chest and let out a heavy sigh. These past two weeks have been incredible and devastating and then incredible again. Everything seems to be going my way these days.

So, of course, I'm worried that right around the corner some horrible nightmare is going to come into my life and ruin everything.

Cade's fingers slowly slide through my hair while I listen to his heartbeat lull me into a state I'd only dreamed of before meeting him. Never in my life have I felt so safe, so protected, and secure. Other women may want the bad boy he probably was before, but not me. I love the feeling of his arms around me as we stand together silently, only the sound of our breathing interrupting the quiet.

"You aren't falling asleep on me, are you?" he whispers against the top of my head.

I smile against his chest and answer, "No. I don't

think I can fall asleep standing up. I'm just loving how relaxed and calm I feel at this moment. Like the world outside can't touch us, and we're safe and sound right here."

His hand cups the back of my head and tilts it back so I'm looking up at him as he stares down at me with dark eyes full of concern. "You're always safe with me, Hailey. I promise that. I won't let anyone hurt you, not even me. I swear."

"I believe you. And I didn't feel safe because we're alone. It's just that this place is so peaceful. Everyday life has no solitude, and when you wrapped your arms around me and I put my head on your chest, I felt more at peace than I can ever remember. You have no idea how much I appreciate that."

He presses a soft kiss to my forehead and lets his lips linger against my skin for a moment before whispering, "I like that I bring you peace. That makes me feel good."

When I close my eyes, I try to think of another human being who has ever made me feel the way Cade does. First he terrified me. Then he intrigued me. When we finally got together, he thrilled me.

And then that night at the club, what I saw shattered me.

But then he did what no one has ever done before with me. He made me want to believe in him again. Believe in us again.

I'm glad I didn't listen to my head when I saw him standing there in the restaurant the other day. All my brain could say was he couldn't be trusted, that he's like all other men.

My heart had a different story to tell. That one said to give him another chance.

This time, my heart was right.

CHAPTER EIGHT

ade

HAILEY SITS BACK ON THE CHAISE LOUNGE NEAR THE pool, and I watch her for a moment as the last yellows and pinks and purples of the sunset fade away. When she told me how relaxed this place made her feel, all I could think about was how I could make her life like that all the time.

I've never felt this way about another soul in the world before her. It's why I can't help but just watch her in the hope that I'll somehow figure out how in such a short time I went from who I was without her to who I am with her.

No wonder my family was betting I'd never find anyone. I barely recognize that Cade from a couple weeks ago. That guy would never have thought to bring a woman here just to spend time together.

Why bother doing that when I have a perfectly good condo with a perfectly good bed?

Yet the moment Hailey asked if we could hang out for a few days so she could stay calm and not freak out about this meeting with that big food blogger, the first thing that popped into my head was taking her away to somewhere quiet and out of town so the two of us could be alone. It was like that was the most natural reaction in the world.

She felt like she was starting to spiral out of control, so I wanted to do whatever I could to stop it. I didn't even think twice.

"Are you watching this gorgeous sunset?" she asks before turning her head to look over at me. "I swear everything in this place is perfect."

"It's like someone painted it for us," I say as I make my way around the pool deck to where she sits.

"Do you want to go swimming?" She giggles and then says, "We could go skinny dipping."

I love how open she is when she says things like that. Looking down at her lying there in her blue tank top and jean shorts, I wonder if any of the neighbors are home.

"Hailey is a skinny dipping girl. Well, now I've heard everything."

She rolls her eyes at my teasing and sits up to kiss me. "I don't look like someone who'd skinny dip?"

I let my gaze roll over her and shake my head. "No, not really. You bake cookies and look too sweet for that."

Hailey's mouth drops open in shock. "And after all

the great sex we've had, you pull that cookie baking good girl thing on me?"

"That's true. Okay, I take it back. You do look like a skinny dipping chick."

She stands up from the chaise lounge and unzips her shorts in front of me. As they fall to the ground, she says, "Well, I'm not because I've never skinny dipped before, but tonight I am. You joining me?"

Before I can get my answer out, she rips her shirt over her head and tosses it on top of her shorts. As I watch in complete surprise, she sheds her bra and panties and then she's standing in front of me and the entire Gulf naked.

"You're way behind, Cade. Catch up. Skinny dipping isn't a solitary sport, you know," Hailey says with a giggle before jumping into the pool.

I don't need to be told twice to get naked for a beautiful woman, so I quickly strip out of my clothes and jump into the water. It's cooler than I expected, but it doesn't take long to get accustomed to it.

"So now we're both skinny dipping people. I think that's one step away from swingers, you know," she says with a playful grin as I make my way over to her.

I kiss her wet lips and smile against them. "I'm not sure I'm ready to be a swinger. That's a whole lifestyle. I think it requires special furniture."

"And special clothes. Easy on and easy off so you don't get caught unprepared when someone wants to get busy," she says so adorably.

Her body presses up against mine, the water lapping around us as we tread water. "You seem to have put some thought into this whole swinger thing. I'm not sure how I feel about sharing you with other guys."

Hailey wraps her arms around my neck and kisses me long and deep. "Mmmm…actually, there's a guy at the restaurant who says he's a swinger, but his hair is all greasy and he combs it over to hide his bald spot, so he might just be saying that."

I can't stop myself from making a face full of disgust just thinking about that greasy guy banging bunches of women. Gross. He's probably in his sixties and hoping to just get some by bragging to someone like Hailey.

Pressing her breasts against me, she nudges her pussy against my cock. "And as for sharing me with other guys," she says and then runs her tongue along the seam of my mouth, "my vote is no on that and that goes twice as much the other way with you and other women. I don't share well with others."

I slide my hands down her back to cup her ass and pull her into me even more. My cock is as hard as steel and getting harder with every time she rolls her hips.

"Good, because I wasn't happy with the idea of you and anyone but me. Glad we got that settled."

She reaches down between us to grip my cock and strokes from base to head once and then twice before kissing me again. "No way I'm sharing this with another woman. No way, no how."

I've had enough foreplay, so I lift her out of the water and position her at the perfect height so I can slide my cock inside that perfect cunt of hers. She looks down at me like some goddess straight from the sea, and when I lower her down onto me, she narrows her eyes to give me that sexy look I love to see when I'm inside her.

"Is your grandmother going to be mad that we're having sex in her pool?" she asks with such innocence to her voice that it feels wrong to be fucking her.

Moving toward the side of the pool, I shake my head. "I don't plan on telling her, to be honest."

I feel the cool tile wall against the base of my spine, so I lean back to brace myself. Hailey rolls her hips again, taking every inch of me, and wraps her legs around my waist.

"Why do I have the feeling you've done this whole pool sex thing before?" I ask and then thrust my hips forward to fill her.

She shakes her head and smiles. "Mmmm…no. Remember? This is my first time skinny dipping. I did read about it, though. You?"

At the moment, I can't think about anything but how good she feels riding my cock with all this water sloshing around between us, so I give her a noncommittal shrug and focus on fucking her. I don't want to remember whoever I had sex with in some guy's pool in high school. None of that means anything to me now.

I pull her mouth to mine and kiss her as every cell in my body screams how fucking good this feels. Her breasts bounce up and down in the water and rub against my skin to send a wave of sensation through me.

Stuffing my hands in her wet hair, I tug hard and she makes a moaning sound into my mouth that I swear goes straight to my cock. "Mmmm...baby, you are the perfect skinny dipper."

Suddenly, Hailey stops moving, and I open my eyes to see her staring up at the deck, her eyes wide and full of something that looks like she's seen a ghost. "Cade—"

She doesn't get another word out before a voice behind me says, "I guess we stopped in at a bad time."

A second later, I spin my head around to see Wilder and two of his friends standing there staring down at us like some kind of asshole Peeping Toms. Hailey practically crawls beneath me to hide, so I push her against the wall of the pool and cover her with my body as I stand up to my full height.

"What are you doing here, Wilder?" I ask, barely able to hide my disgust at seeing him standing there.

"Just came over to hang out for a little while. My father said the place was empty, so he didn't see why it would be a problem," he answers in his usual snide tone.

"Well, your father was wrong, obviously. Why don't you and your friends go back the way you came in? We're here for the next few days."

I look down and see Hailey cringing at every moment she has to stand there naked. "Cade, who are these people?"

"My cousin and his friends," I say to her and then look back up at Wilder. "And they're leaving. Now."

One of his friends who looks a little older than me

cranes his neck to look down into the pool and grins. "I'm always up for a gang bang. What about you guys?"

Barely able to contain my rage on most occasions with my cousin, now I want to tear his head off and both his buddies' heads. "Get them the fuck out of here, Wilder. And try finding a better class of friends than a scumbag like that one."

The asshole with the smart mouth starts to cock off, but Wilder understands now's not the time to be playing with me. I don't care if I have to climb out of this fucking water buck naked and kick their asses before I dry off. No punk ass friend of my least favorite cousin is going to talk about my girlfriend like that.

I glare up at Wilder, and it doesn't take long before he gets the idea. "Let's go. We can hang out somewhere else."

Both of his friends take one last look at Hailey and me and shrug before walking away. When they're all inside, I look down at her and let out a heavy sigh. "And that's Wilder, the world's worst cock block, ladies and gentleman. I'm sorry about that. He's bad enough, but his friends are always pure assholes. Are you okay?"

"I'm fine. I just didn't know what to do when I saw them standing there watching us," she says. "So that's another one of your family members? I hope you don't mind me saying I like Alex better than this one."

Nodding, I can't disagree with that. "Everyone

does. Alex is a good time. Wilder's nothing but sulky bullshit and trouble."

With a smile, she says, "Not that I got a really good look before you hid me away, thank you very much for that, by the way, but he doesn't look like you and Alex. I think I just assumed you guys would all look alike."

I hear the downstairs door finally slam shut and breathe a sigh of relief. I didn't have beating the hell out of Wilder and his jackass friends with my dick hanging out on my schedule today.

"That's because he's adopted, although, he sort of looks a little like my uncle Kane, strangely enough. Most of us look like Alex and me. Brown hair, brown eyes, you know—like us. But Liam and Cash look like that side of the family with dark hair and blue eyes. It's just a coincidence that Wilder looks like them, I guess. Enough talking about him. Let's get back to what we were doing."

As I move to nuzzle Hailey's neck, she pushes me away, shaking her head. "I can't, Cade. That was definitely a mood killer."

Fucking Wilder. Add this to the million other reasons I can't stand him.

Trying not to sulk, I nod and force a smile. "I get it. Well, since they're gone, we can get out and dry off before we get something to eat. How's that sound?"

She cradles my face and kisses me sweetly, which only makes me want what she doesn't even more. "Thank you for understanding. That just freaked me out a little. Maybe it's because it's my first time skinny dipping?"

I can't help but laugh at how cute she is. Lifting her out of the pool, I let myself enjoy the view of her body with the water droplets rolling off her tan skin. Fucking Wilder and his friends.

"You were doing fine at your first time until my cousin loped in here. Blame it on him."

Hailey hands me a towel from the bin on the other side of the desk, and her eyes wander down my body before she looks up at me with a smile. "I was having a very good time. I hope you know that."

"I do."

"And I loved how you protected me and made them go away. I was worried you might have to get out of the pool and fight them," she says with worry hanging off every word. "It would have been three-on-one."

"And me with my dick hanging out," I joke as I knot the towel at my hip. "But Wilder wouldn't have let it get that far. There's no love lost between the two of us, but he's part of the family, so he would have stopped his friends. Or I would have put on a show for you and hope you liked men who do their best ancient Greco-Roman wrestling imitation."

Hailey's eyes narrow, and she shakes her head. "Your what?"

"Nothing. Just something I saw on TV the other day. Back in ancient times, the men wrestled naked."

A look of surprise settles into her expression.

"Really. Now I'm going to have that image in my head all night."

I pull her to me and kiss her, wishing we were still in the pool. "I think I'll try to give you something else to think about."

"Even better," she says, giving me one of those Hailey smiles that lights up her face and makes her so beautiful.

CHAPTER NINE

ade

BACKING OUT OF THE GARAGE FROM THE ISLAND house, I wish Hailey and I never had to leave this place. Other than my cousin and his asshole friends crashing our party that first night, we spent the next two days lying around adoring one another and having sex. That was it, except for a few times we got out of bed to put some food into our stomachs.

Hailey leans over and kisses me softly on the cheek. "Thank you for these last few days, Cade. They were just what I needed. Today, I'm going to go into the restaurant and I'm going to start making the best desserts I've ever made."

As we drive away, I thread my fingers through hers and step on the gas. "And I'm going to bartend this weekend and wish I was sitting at the restaurant trying out all the desserts you're making."

"Do you have to work all weekend?"

I hear the disappointment in her voice come through loud and clear. I know how she feels. I'm disappointed I have to work too. I'd much rather spend my time eating cookies and cakes and then falling asleep with her next to me in bed.

Forcing a smile, I nod as I make a turn onto the main road. "All weekend. Sunday the club isn't open, but I know he's going to be having me do inventory or some damn thing." I look over at her as I bring her hand up to my mouth to kiss it. "But come Monday, I'll be at Comfort Food ready to see all those incredible desserts you came up with this weekend. I promise."

Like always, her face lights up when she talks about what she creates. "I really want to wow her on Friday. I hope I can come up with something amazing."

"You will, and then maybe you'll get people to start paying you what you deserve for your creations."

"Oh, I don't know about that. I just want more people to hear about my parents' restaurant and come in to help their business. That's why I do this. They've been so incredible all my life but especially this past year, Cade. I just want to help them out, and since this is the best way I know to do it, I want to show Brooke Dunning how great the desserts are so she'll tell her fans to come to the restaurant."

I kiss her hand and smile over at her. "I know you will. Don't worry. You got this."

Worry comes off her in waves, though, so the whole way back home, I tell her stories about the March and Jackson clan and the trouble we all used to get into. Nothing makes people laugh more than the idiocy of teenage boys and the messes they cause, and at least for a little while, she doesn't think about all the importance she's put on this podcast with the food lady.

When I pull the car into the Comfort Food parking lot, I'm sorry we had to return to the city so soon. I could spend a month out at the island house, away from everything and everyone but her.

"Thanks for bringing me to the restaurant. I want to get started working on things immediately. Call me when you have time. I know you have to work and you probably usually sleep late the day after, but when you have a chance…"

Gently pulling her to me, I kiss her lips to stop her from talking. "You don't have to worry. I'll wake up early to call. I got up early the other day to come over here to convince you to take me back, so I can do it again."

Hailey gives me a tiny smile and nods. "Okay. Should I tell you to have fun at work? Is it fun?" she asks with trepidation in her voice.

She's thinking about what she saw that night with Kylie. I need to do whatever I can to make her understand that is not what my job is supposed to be, and after that little talk with my father the other day, that won't be what my job is ever again.

I somberly shake my head. "It's anything but fun. I'd rather be with you on my balcony or anywhere else in the world with you instead of screaming over the music asking drunks what they want."

A tiny smile brightens her face. "Okay, then. Don't have fun. Save the fun for the next time I see you after the weekend," she says. "We'll do something fun on Monday night."

Her cheeks turn pink, and she adds, "Maybe I'll read a few chapters of one of my favorite books and see what I can come up with."

I love how sexy she is, even when she's talking about reading. Definitely the first time I've ever associated that with anything hot.

"Okay. You have fun this weekend. Love you."

Pressing her forehead to mine, she smiles. "I love you too. See you Monday!"

When she jumps out of the car and runs toward the front door of the restaurant, I watch her and can't help wish I didn't have to be stuck in the club tonight doing the thing I hate most in life. Just before she walks inside, she turns around and waves and then blows me a kiss.

I don't think any woman other than my mother has ever blown me a kiss in my life. I instantly love it because it's from Hailey.

· · ·

GRABBING MY PHONE, I CALL ALEX AS I'M LEAVING the parking lot. "Hey, where are you? Are you at work already or at your place?"

"I'm the early shift today, so I'm at work already. Why? I thought you and Hailey were hanging out at the Anna Maria Island house until later today," he says over the noise of the kitchen around him.

"We were, but we left early. She wants to get to work on what she's going to make for that blogger when she does her podcast next Friday, but I think fucking Wilder crashing in on us the first night freaked her out too."

Alex laughs like he always does when something frustrates me. I think he finds amusement in my unhappiness somehow.

"Wilder did what? Why did he go out there?" he asks over some whirring sound that reminds me of a broken drill.

"Dude, I can barely hear you. What the hell do you people do in that kitchen? I thought you cooked food. Why does it sound like you're standing in an auto body shop?" I ask as I head toward CK.

"Shit doesn't happen like magic, Cade," he snaps.

He gets like that when I comment on his job or how he performs it. So fucking touchy.

"Prep is noisy, man. What can I say?"

"Well, say you have a couple minutes to talk since I'm driving to the restaurant right now."

He doesn't say anything, but the ruckus in the background gets loud enough with some mixer now on that he finally yells into my ear, "Yeah, I can talk for a few. Come to the back door. Kane or my father will let you in since we aren't open yet."

Fifteen minutes later, I'm banging on that metal door for the third time and wondering if the noisy prep means no one will ever hear me out here. I pound my fist against the door one more time, and then it flies open to reveal Alex standing there looking irritated.

"What?" I ask as I walk by him. "I didn't think anyone heard me so I kept knocking."

Behind me, he mumbles, "It sounded like you were using a battering ram."

I look back at him and see his expression is miserable. His eyebrows are all drawn in toward his nose, and his frown looks like it's found a permanent place on his face. Alex isn't usually like this, even when he's peeved about me commenting on his job.

"What's up? You look like someone just ran over your best friend, which can't be the case since I'm standing here just fine."

He waves away my question, shaking his head as he pushes past me. "Nothing. So what happened with Wilder out at the house?"

I follow him to the kitchen, not sure how we're going to talk now if we couldn't do it on the phone because of all the noise, but surprisingly, it doesn't sound like an auto body shop now. Alex points at a spot in the corner nearby and walks a few feet away to a metal table where what looks like a bushel of carrots waits for him.

"That's a lot of carrots," I say with a chuckle. "You guys getting a family of rabbits for lunch today?"

He simply rolls his eyes and picks up a knife to begin chopping the orange vegetables. "Fuck you. Now what happened with Wilder?"

Remembering his father could be anywhere nearby, I ask, "Where's Kane?"

Alex waves away yet another of my questions and gets back to chopping. "He left about ten minutes ago. You're fine."

"You know how he is about Wilder. I didn't want to get into that. As for our fantastic cousin, he brought two of his friends to the house and the fuckers walked right in and caught Hailey and me skinny dipping in the pool."

With a smile, Alex says, "I didn't have her pegged for a skinny dipping chick. I like that. So what happened when they saw you guys buck naked in the water?"

"The fuckers just stood there. One of them even fucking mentioned a gang bang. Asshole. I thought I was going to have to get out of the pool and fight them. Seriously, where does he find his friends? My car was parked out front. It's not like he doesn't know what I drive. He knew I was there and still came in with those two shitheads."

Looking over at me, Alex winces. "How did Hailey take all of this?"

"She was freaked out and rightfully so. Nothing like us having a good time and her looking up to see him and two guys staring down into the pool like we were giving the world a fucking peep show. I had to threaten them before he thought it was a good idea to leave."

After tossing the chopped up vegetables into a bowl, he pulls another pile of carrots in front of him and starts cutting them. "Sounds like him. I bet he didn't even ask Grandma before he just busted into the place. What were the three stooges planning to do there? Take a swim?"

I shake my head at that idea. "No way. Those two he was with looked like they were straight out of some dive. They were probably looking for some place to party. Two million dollar house and he brings that garbage to hang out there."

Behind me, a voice says, "You two finished talking shit, or do you want to continue?"

No sooner do the words filter through my brain, I'm spinning around to face Wilder himself. "Have a nice time the other night? Maybe I can invite you over to my place so you can watch my girlfriend and me fuck? Bring your friends and we can make it a party," I say with disgust just having to look at him.

"You mean like a gang bang? You didn't seem to be a fan the other night. Either did your girlfriend."

A second later, I lunge at him, slamming him into some metal rack that makes a horrible clanging noise when it crashes into the wall behind it. I've wanted to beat the hell out of this asshole for years, and that little crack is going to get him what he deserves.

What I've been holding back for far too long.

He's a little bigger than I am after his time in prison, but he isn't carrying the rage for me that I have for him. That I've had for so long I can barely see straight sometimes when I have to listen to everyone talk about how great it is that he's getting his life back together and how wonderful it is that he's making the most of his second chance.

Wilder is an asshole who gets away with all kinds of shit in our family and has all his life. Today, that ends, at least with me.

I get a few good punches in before he hits me hard in the side, taking most of the wind out of my lungs. Stunned, I stagger back, but my anger helps me regroup in only a second or two, not enough time for him to take advantage.

He moves to take my legs out from under me, but I grab him around his chest and push him back into the wall. The metal rack and the few utensils left hanging on it make that loud, clanging noise again, and I hear him grunt when he runs up against it.

I don't know when Cassian and Kane show up to pull us apart, but I feel someone's arms wrap around my shoulders and yank me off Wilder, and a second later, I look up to see Kane doing the same with his son.

"Cut it out!" Cassian barks in my ear. "Cut this shit out now, you two! What the hell are you doing brawling in my kitchen?" he asks.

Neither Wilder nor I answer his question. Instead, the two of us struggle to shake off the men holding us so we can get back to fighting.

"Enough!" Kane bellows. "That's enough!"

Behind me, Cassian angrily says in my ear, "You come with me. I want to talk to you."

Reaching out to grab Wilder as my uncle pushes me out of the kitchen, I snap, "I'm not done with him yet. Get off me! Let me go!"

Cassian tightens his hold on me and forces me out into the hallway and down to the office he shares with Kane. He kicks the door open and thrusts me into the room before pointing at the chair next to his desk.

"Don't say one fucking word until I sit down. My head is pounding, and it isn't even noon yet."

ade

WHEN HE FLOPS DOWN ONTO HIS CHAIR, CASSIAN takes a deep breath in and lets it out slowly, like he needs to calm himself down before we have this talk he so desperately wants to have with me. After a few seconds, I begin to speak, but he holds up his hand and shakes his head, a clear sign he isn't ready yet.

"Not one fucking word."

"You're already sitting down. I figured I could start talking now."

His blue eyes flash an anger rarely seen in my uncle recently. "Don't be a smart ass. You know what I meant."

"Actually, I don't know why I'm here getting this treatment while that asshole is probably out in the dining room having a little snack to soothe his feelings."

Cassian takes another breath in and lets it out before asking, "What is with you two? You nearly came to blows on Labor Day last year, and at Christmas your grandmother thought the two of you were going to tear up her living room. This is the third time one of us has had to step in and separate you two. So what's going on?"

My heartbeat begins to slow down and return to normal now that the adrenaline isn't pumping through my body. Sagging in my chair, I look away, not wanting to have this conversation with this uncle or anyone else.

"Maybe you shouldn't separate us and we can see how that goes."

"What is going on, Cade? All of you boys used to hang out in school. You never fought then. What's happened in the past year to make you two always want to be at each other's throats?" Cassian asks, genuinely not knowing why I've had a problem with Wilder for a long time.

Long before he showed up and he and his friends acted like dicks to Hailey.

I turn to look at my uncle and see real concern in his expression. Always the brother who wanted a big, happy family, he's bothered when any of us don't get along. By the look in his eyes now, I have a feeling he's really freaked out by what he just saw.

He has no idea how long it was in coming.

"As for why he has a problem with me, I have no

idea. I haven't had a conversation with him since like eleventh grade. So you're going to have to ask him about that. As for me, my problem with Wilder is what it's been since we were kids. This past year just brought it into sharper focus."

Cassian nods, but I doubt he knows what's going on. He probably thinks it has to do with Wilder getting sent away for a year. I don't care about that. People do stupid things like stealing stuff. Wilder has always done things like that. He just happened to get caught this time.

And just as I guessed, my uncle quietly asks, "Is this about him going to jail? Everybody makes mistakes, Cade. He's family. We're supposed to support him now that he's out."

Just hearing that same tired excuse for that shithead's bad behavior makes me want to throw up. "To be honest, Cassian, I don't care about that. It was pretty inevitable that Wilder was going to end up in jail at some point or another. I mean, come on. He was trouble from the minute he showed up in our family. Was anyone really surprised that he got caught stealing money from someone? Really? But I don't care about that. What pisses me off is he always gets a fucking pass. He fails a grade? Oh, he'll do better next year and we all have to support him. He gets in trouble with the cops the first time? Oh, well he's had a troubled life. He gets in trouble with the cops the next five times? Same excuse. Every goddamned time it's 'he's had a rough life.' Fuck that. He's had a charmed life with Kane and

Abbi, and I don't know why anyone wants to pretend otherwise."

The shocked look on my uncle's face tells me he had no idea I harbored these feelings for my cousin. Oh, well. Now the truth is out. I'm sure he'll try to give me some lecture on how Wilder's life has been so tough, but I'm not buying it.

"What is all of this really about, Cade? You don't care for your cousin, but not because of him getting in trouble or even that we all are probably a little too easy on him. But that's not what this is about, is it?"

Part of me wants to stand up, toss this chair I'm sitting on across the room, and storm out of this place since he just admitted what I've known forever and it doesn't seem to bother him. But another part of me is finally ready to say what's been on my mind about Wilder and his bullshit.

Congratulations, Cassian March. You're the lucky guy who gets to hear what I have to say today. Buckle up. It's going to get pretty fucking wild from this point on.

I lean forward toward his desk and take a deep breath, but not to calm myself down like he did a few minutes ago. I need that air in my lungs so I can get all these fucking words out I've been holding in for what feels like forever.

"You know what this is all about? I've been busting my balls being everything I was supposed to be, and when I want to take some time to figure out just what the fuck I want to do with my life, I get nothing but grief about it. Wilder, on the other hand, gets to screw up time after time after time, and nobody gives him a hassle about a single goddamned thing."

My uncle opens his mouth to say something, but I'm not done yet, so I hold up my hand to stop him. "I got great grades in high school and never failed a damn class. He failed a whole entire grade. But did anyone give him a moment's grief about it? Nope. When I graduated, I was expected to go to college, but he gets a pass because everyone is just happy he got out. I go to a top rate school and do well for four years. And what did he do in that time? He got caught stealing and got sent to prison. So then last year the two of us were fresh off college and doing time. Has he spent the last year being asked what he's going to do with his life? Is he expected to hold down even a part-time job? No on both counts."

And now comes the part that pisses me off the most.

"I never fucked up the way he did. Never. Yet I get the 'Cade, you need to have a job or you'll lose everything' speech from my father, while that son of a bitch gets to do exactly what he wants to do or doesn't want to do and nobody says a damn word to him. That's why he can bust up into the island house the other night with his two lowlife friends he probably met in jail while I'm there with my girlfriend and he has to be fucking told to leave. So yeah, it's not really about one thing. It's about a lifetime of things that he's gotten away with while I don't get a damn pass on anything."

When the last word comes out of my mouth, it

feels like a ten ton weight has been lifted off me. I lean back against the chair and take another deep breath, blowing it out in a rush a second later.

That felt good. All of it. Saying what's on my mind. Not holding back. Everything.

Cassian looks like he's been slapped across the face when I finish, leaning back in his own chair like he needs to increase the space between us just in case I start talking again. He doesn't have to worry. I've got nothing more to say about the subject of my cousin and how goddamned easy he's had it all his life.

"Cade, I had no idea you were dealing with so much," he says quietly, like he's in shock after what I just told him. "I know your father means well, but I don't think he realizes the pressure he's put on you all this time."

I shake my head, not willing to let my father take the blame for everything this time. "It's not that, though. I never cared about his expectations. Well, not until recently now that he's shanghaied me back into service at the club. But it never bothered me that I was expected to do well in school and go to college and do well there too. All of us dealt with that. Alex wasn't given a pass on anything by you and Olivia. Neither was Cash. Liam either, which is strange since he's got the same parents as Wilder. It wasn't just me who was expected to do something, but then you look at how he's gotten away with so much and doesn't have to deal with a single thing, other than when the state decided he needed to do some time for taking that money. This isn't about my father and me. It's about two men with a single year yet only one of them has to get his life entirely planned out while the other has all the freedom in the world."

"He did have a rough start, Cade. His mother overdosed when he was five, and if it hadn't been for Kane and Abbi, he would have been on a path to surely repeat his mother's mistake."

I point across the desk at him when he proves exactly what I've been talking about. "That. That right there. He was five when that happened. Since then, he's been with our family and gotten to enjoy all the good stuff the rest of us have. When exactly does something that happened to him twenty years ago stop being an excuse for the rest of his life?"

Cassian hangs his head, unable to answer that question just like everyone else in our family. "I'm sorry you're unhappy working for your father, Cade. For what it's worth, I don't think he intends it as a punishment. I don't think he'd want your life to be unhappy like this."

"You don't get it. I'm not unhappy. I have a girlfriend I'm crazy about. I love my condo and my car. My best friend, who is probably still stunned I tried to go all MMA in his kitchen, and most of my family are great. So I'm happy. I just have a hard time swallowing the insistence that I figure out what I want to do with the rest of my life when Wilder, who is two years older than me and has already done time, gets to live life how he wants and bust up a night with my girlfriend at the island house with his two scumbag friends because he has no responsibilities."

"I'm not going to ask what happened there. Just tell me your grandmother's house doesn't look like the wreck you made of the kitchen a few minutes ago," Cassian says in a voice full of worry to match the panicked expression he's giving me.

The way he makes it seem like Wilder and I are the same kind of man pisses me off. I fold my arms across my chest and shake my head as I push down the urge to tell my favorite uncle to fuck off.

"I wouldn't do that to Grandma's house, Cassian. Can you say the same for him?"

He doesn't answer, which tells me all I need to know. He isn't blind to what Wilder is. Good. Now maybe he can act like it from now on.

Standing to leave, I look toward the door for the first time, remembering that Kane is nearby and might have heard everything I said. Too bad. I'm tired of pretending just for family unity and peace.

Cassian looks up at me and tries to give me a sympathetic smile. "Do you want me to talk to your father? He probably doesn't realize any of this is happening with you, so it might help if I spoke to him."

"Not necessary. My father knows perfectly well how I feel about being back at Club X. And just so everyone in this family doesn't get it wrong about me, I'm not there because I'm lazy or I can't get another job. I don't know what I want to do, but since my father demanded I work at something or lose everything that's mine, I chose to go back there. I hate it, but I don't have another choice right now."

My uncle doesn't say anything for a long moment, but then a smile lifts the corners of his mouth until he gives me a big Cassian March grin that could charm the birds out of the trees. "I sometimes forget how much you're like Stefan. I can't tell you how many times he said something very similar about your uncle back when he was close to your age. You might even find he agrees with you when it comes to Wilder. He just can't see it because he's too busy being your father."

"Well, feel free to clue him into that. I don't need you to talk to him about me or what I'm doing with my life, though. He knows already. He sees me five nights a week behind the main bar."

"Do you mind me giving you some advice I gave your father all those years ago?"

The last thing I want is advice about anything concerning how I feel about Wilder at this moment, but since I doubt it would matter if I said no, I merely give him a noncommittal shrug. I know how this family works. If he doesn't say it to me, I'm likely to get a call from someone else looking to share their wisdom about this topic with me. Better to hear it from Cassian since I like him the most out of nearly everyone, except his sons.

"Don't let resentment about this eat you up. It will steal your happiness, and you don't deserve to have that happen."

I look down at him, unconvinced he ever said that to his younger brother. "You told my father that? In those words?"

He laughs and leans back in his chair. "Well, I probably sprinkled in a few expletives and called him a name or two, but it was basically the same sentiment."

"And what was his response?" I ask, now curious about how that little talk went compared to how I'm feeling right now.

"I don't recall specifically what he said, but I imagine it involved telling me to fuck off or to mind my own business. You know your father when he gets hot about something."

"That I do," I say as I move to leave.

"Come back again," he says as I head toward the door. "But next time, don't bust up my kitchen, okay?"

I give him a nod and force a smile for my favorite uncle. "I'll see what I can do."

If Wilder's there, I can't promise anything. Just because I admitted how pissed off he gets me doesn't mean I won't want to take a swing at him the next time he shows up in front of my face.

CHAPTER ELEVEN

ailey

ALL WEEKEND, I TRIED OUT NEW RECIPES IN MY quest to find the very best desserts to show off to Brooke Dunning. The Boston Cream Whoopie Pies with chocolate glaze turned out incredible, so they definitely made the cut. The coconut and pistachio meringue cookies didn't end up as good, though, but I might try again this week before I meet her on Friday. My tried and true key lime pie came through like always, but I'm not sure I want to take something so commonplace to a meeting with a nationally known food blogger.

All of this fills my head on Monday afternoon when my phone rings with a call from Cade. Thrilled to speak to him for the first time since Saturday afternoon, I quickly answer and start talking without even saying hi.

"Wait until you see what I came up with! I'm still working on a couple more, but I saved you a whoopie pie you're going to love."

"I hope it can keep until tomorrow afternoon. I have to fill in for Katelyn tonight," he says, sounding disappointed.

And I have to make it worse when I tell him I can't see him then either. "I have to work on these every day, Cade. I'm sorry. How about Tuesday night?"

"She can't work until Thursday, so that's the first night I'll be off. Any chance that pie is going to be good three days from now?"

"Probably not," I sulk. "But I have to make more for Friday, so I can save you one of those. I'm going to miss you this week."

"Me too, Hailey. I miss you already, and it's only been a couple days since I've seen you."

He sounds so down that I want to do something to cheer him up. "Well, think about what you want to do on Thursday night and we'll go all out. Whatever you want. I'm going to need something to take the stress away because I'm probably going to be pretty strung out by then. I just hope I find some more desserts that work."

I hear a smile in his voice when he says, "You will. Don't worry. As for Thursday, we're probably not going to leave the bedroom. I miss you so much already."

My cheeks heat up as I blush at the thought of

how much I wish we could be together right now. "I'm fine with that. We just have to make sure we bring in some drinks. Hydration is key in marathons," I say with a giggle.

"I'll stock up on some because I'm going to be in marathon mode by the time Thursday rolls around."

"Good. That'll make two of us."

I sense unhappiness creep into our conversation again when he falls silent, but before I can try to cheer him up with a funny story about how one of my chocolate creations blew up in my face, covering me from my neck up in melted chocolate, he clears his throat and says, "I have to go. Katelyn shows up earlier than I do because she handles the upkeep of the main bar usually, so now that's on me. I'll call you tomorrow, okay. Or maybe I'll text you tonight if it's not too busy."

The way he sounds makes me wonder if he's just miserable about going to work at the club or something else. I don't know how to ask about what that something else may be, though.

"Okay. I'm always up for texts."

"Then maybe I'll send some if I can."

Everything about him sounds so noncommittal now. Has something changed between us, I wonder?

"Is there anything you want to talk about, Cade?"

"No. I'm the same old me. Just not looking forward to work tonight. I wanted to see you instead of a bunch of drunks. Everything's okay, and I promise by Thursday night, I'll be out of this funk."

"Okay. I'll miss you."

"Me too, Hailey. Talk to you later."

When the call ends, I can't help question if there's something else that's wrong. He was so happy all those days we spent together. Now he sounds like a different person.

I shake my head to push those needless worries out of my head. He doesn't like his job. That's it. It's nothing more.

"KNOCK KNOCK! CAN YOU HAVE VISITORS?"

Lifting my head from a lump of dough that refuses to do what I want, I smile at the sight of Meadow and Alex standing in front of me. "Hi! You're the last two people I expected to see tonight."

I quickly wipe my hands on my stained apron I've been wearing all day and hope I don't have flour or anything else on my face. "What are you guys doing here?"

"When Meadow said you were hunkered down here coming up with new desserts, I told her I wanted to come over and check them out. You don't mind us intruding, do you?" Alex says, seeming genuinely concerned about interrupting me.

"You're always welcome in this kitchen. Both of you. It's almost closing time, so it's just me back here anyway. I'm hoping to stumble upon something incredible, but so far, no luck. I should have stopped playing with this dough half an hour ago. Now it's just a mess."

Meadow gives me a wide-eyed stare and glances

over at Alex to let me know she's thrilled to be hanging out with him tonight. I wish I could ask her how it all came about, but since the restaurant is basically closed, I have no reason to be dragging her off to the dining room without him knowing we're gossiping about him.

"Any chance you have anything hanging around I can do a taste test on?" he asks with a sly smile.

"I have a Boston Cream Whoopie Pie I think might change your life," I joke and then point over toward the rack behind him.

He and Meadow turn around and let out audible gasps. "Hailey, it's huge!" Meadow says. "No one person can eat that and live."

"Then it's perfect for sharing."

The two of them grab forks and knives and dig in to taste what has of yet been my best creation for my meeting with Brooke Dunning. "You two enjoy. I'll be right back. I want to grab some strawberries for an idea that just came to me."

By the time I return from the refrigerator, the whoopie pie is gone. Coming around the corner, I spy Meadow wiping chocolate from Alex's chin and I can't help but smile. They really are cute together.

"So how did that taste?" I ask as I sit down and place the case of strawberries on the table in front of me.

"Incredible. I would eat your desserts every day if you'd agree to come work at CK," Alex says, licking his lips of the last hint of chocolate on them.

"Honey, you are going to be single-handedly

keeping dentists in business in this town with treats like that," Meadow says with a laugh.

I smile at her, remembering what Brooke said after she ate the apple tarts the other day. "And gyms too. The woman I'm meeting with said she needed to take three extra spin classes after indulging in the dessert she had here that day, and those were only apple tarts. What do you think what you guys just had would require? A week or two of those classes?" I ask with a chuckle.

"At least," she says. "Who is this woman? Does she look like she takes that many spin classes? I guess I always pictured food bloggers to be a softer lot since they spend all their time with food."

My attention turns to Alex, who at the moment looks confused by Meadow's idea on people who work in our industry. "I admit I might be a little soft, but I don't think he could be called soft by any stretch of the imagination."

Before he can say anything, Meadow quickly tries to clean up her statement. Shaking her head, she says, "Oh, no. That's not what I meant. I don't think either of you are soft. No, no. I just meant I guess I thought food bloggers were."

Alex and I look at her, neither one of us smiling, and she says, "Maybe I'll just stop. How about those Rays? They played yesterday and looked pretty good. Don't you think?"

I try not to smile, but Alex simply shakes his head and rolls his eyes. "Smooth. So Hailey, what are you doing with the strawberries?"

Happy the subject has changed, Meadow asks, "Yeah, those strawberries look huge. What are you doing with them?"

Lifting one out of the case, I hold it up in front of me. "Well, most people go for dipping strawberries in chocolate. I'm not against that idea since I'm a huge chocolate fan, as you can tell by the whoopie pie you guys just enjoyed, but I wanted to come up with something different. I've tried strawberries dipped in honey and peppercorns, but I was thinking that I'd play around and maybe try chili powder or something equally as spicy. You get the heat but you get the sweet too."

"Or cayenne pepper," Alex suggests excitedly. "That's sounds good."

"I might throw in some lemon juice to see how that picks up the flavors," I explain as the two of them nod.

"You think of the most interesting stuff. I would never even consider mixing those ingredients, but now that you're talking about it, I think I'd want to try it," Meadow says.

"I just want to impress this woman. If she likes what I make, then maybe people will start to finally come in to try my desserts. Then my parents can benefit, like I always intended in the first place."

Meadow's phone rings, and when she takes a look at who's calling, she apologizes for having to take it. "I'll just be a minute. I wouldn't answer this call, but it's a client who's been giving me a hard time, and being new at the firm means I can't lose anyone. I'll be right back."

She hurries out to the dark dining room, leaving Alex and me alone. I want to ask him about Cade after that phone call with him left me wondering if anything's wrong, but I don't know how to broach the subject. He might not even know either.

Still, I have his best friend standing in front of me, so I can't let go of the chance to find out.

"Have you spoken to Cade at all in the last couple days?" I ask in a quiet voice as I focus on the strawberries and hope I don't sound too pathetic.

"Not since the other day," he says, not sounding like he wants to continue this conversation.

I look up at him to see his expression and notice he doesn't appear uncomfortable. Maybe he really has nothing to say about Cade.

"The last time I saw him he was attempting to beat the hell out of our cousin Wilder in the middle of my kitchen."

Alex's voice holds little emotion, but what he's saying sounds like it should. I know I'd be furious if people came into my kitchen and stared a brawl near where I was working.

"Why would he do that? Is he okay? He didn't seem right when I talked to him a little while ago. Maybe that's why."

Alex shrugs, as if all of this is perfectly normal and he's seen it a hundred times before with his best friend. "He and Wilder don't get along. I'm not sure they ever have. Not that I blame Cade. I'm not a big fan of Wilder either. But don't worry. Cade got the best of him before my father and uncle broke them up."

I think back to that night at the house on the island and remember Wilder was the name of the person who interrupted us in the pool. "I think I met this Wilder person. He and two of his friends came by your grandmother's house out on Anna Maria Island when we were there. Cade was pretty frosty with him, but I thought it was just because he walked in on us."

"Just the most recent straw that broke the camel's back, I'm guessing," Alex says. "They aren't close like he and I are. In fact, Wilder's not close to any of us, even his own brother. So it's not only Cade who has a problem with him."

The way Alex defends his best friend makes me smile. "Well, I was worried they were going to get into a fight that night out at the house. I guess I shouldn't be surprised that it happened, but in your kitchen? You must have been livid."

"I'm passionate about a lot of things, including my job and my kitchen. I understand other people don't see why, but they're passionate about their own stuff. It was bound to happen at some point. The situation between them just boiled over that day. It's not like they planned to bust up my workplace."

"Was it because Wilder and his friends came to the house when we were there?" I ask, still trying to figure out what's changed with Cade to make him sound so different on the phone when we talked earlier.

Alex nods, giving me a tiny smile I sense is to make what he has to say about his best friend easier for me to hear. "That and a bunch of other things. Cade's under a lot of pressure from our family to decide what he wants to do with his life. I think it's unfair, to be honest. He isn't like me. I've known what I want to do since I was a kid. He isn't that way. Then he sees our cousin two years older than him and not knowing what he's going to do with his life and nobody says a word about it. I think it finally just got to him."

"I like how he is. He's smart and funny, and I'm sure when he finds what he wants to do, he'll be all in on it. Having your whole life planned out isn't as good as everyone thinks either. I thought I knew what I wanted to do and that didn't turn out. Now I'm making desserts in my parents' restaurant when three years ago I could barely microwave soup."

Forcing a smile to hide my true feelings about the memories of what brought me to this point in life, I point down at the strawberries, suddenly uncomfortable with talking about this subject. "And tonight, I get to do fabulous things with strawberries. I definitely didn't need to get a degree in psychology to do that."

"I agree with you. Cade's a free spirit, and everyone trying to pin him down on something only makes him want to rebel. When he finds something he loves, he'll go head first into it. That's how he is. He can go from zero to hundred percent once he decides he wants something. You're proof of that. Just a few weeks ago, you two didn't even know each other. Now, you're all he thinks of. When he finds what he wants to do in life, he'll be the same way. He does nothing halfway."

His mention of how Cade is with me makes me

blush, and I look away to avoid his gaze. I don't know how much his friend has told him about us, but I hope he's left out some of the sexier details. I'm not sure I could face Alex if he knew everything.

Like skinny dipping with Cade at his grandmother's house, for example. Or the specifics of our sex life.

Thankfully, Meadow returns before the silence between us grows truly awkward, and I'm thankful she doesn't pick up on it. "So that client is going to make me age overnight, you know that? I have to get to the office. I'm sorry to bail on you, Alex."

"Perfectly fine," he says with a smile. "I understand being on for the job. Hailey and I were just talking about that. I'll take you back home so you can get to work right now."

Turning to face me, Meadow asks, "Are you going to be okay here alone? Your father and everyone else is gone already. I feel terrible us leaving you here like this."

I wave away her concern, truly not worried about being the only person in the restaurant after hours. It's not the first time, and I doubt it will be the last time.

"Nonsense. Go take over the design world. I need to figure out what I want to do with these strawberries, so it's no problem. I'll see you guys later."

After they leave, I think about what Alex said about Cade and smile. I like how he's someone who can dive into something he's interested in and become engrossed by that thing. Or that person. Other women might not like how he can go from zero to one hundred percent in no time, but for someone like me who wasn't sure she'd ever be able to trust another man, that's exactly what I need.

I just hope he isn't changing his mind.

CHAPTER TWELVE

ade

DURING A LULL ON AN UNUSUALLY BUSY MONDAY night, I see Alex poke his head out of the crowd at the front bar and wave me down to him. It's not like him to be out at a club on a weeknight. He's like a kid who's always good in school—weeknights are for doing good stuff, not trolling the bar at Club X.

"What the hell are you doing here?" I ask with a smile. "Isn't it after your bedtime on a school night?"

An eye roll and a fuck you are what I get in return. "I just came from hanging out with your girlfriend. She's working hard at coming up with some great things for her meeting this week. I got to try a whoopie pie that might have sent me into sugar shock, but damn, it was worth it."

That should have been my whoopie pie. If I hadn't

been called in to sub for Katelyn, I'd be with Hailey right now enjoying all sorts of things, including one of her delicious desserts.

"Yeah? Must be nice. So did you come over to rub it in my face?" I ask as I scan the bar for any customers who need a drink.

"No. Just making conversation. You planning on trying to kick my ass too? Is it some kind of thing you're doing, getting into fights with every male member of your family? Cash and Liam aren't here, so you can't get a three-for-one thing going on."

Alex is unusually snappy tonight, and I turn to see his gaze leveled on me pretty aggressively. That's not like him. What the hell is going on?

"What's up with you?" I ask, leaning forward to see him close up.

He lightens up instantly, shrugging away my question. "Nothing. Just frustrated. Give me a Jack and Coke, and go light on the soda."

I mix his drink and set it down in front of him before waiting on some guy who looks like he's going to burst if he doesn't get some alcohol in his system in the next sixty seconds. When I get back to Alex a few minutes later, half his drink is gone. That's definitely not like him. Something must be really frustrating him tonight.

"So do you want to tell me what's making you into an alcoholic, or do I have to do my best bartender routine and let you gradually confess what's wrong? I'm here all night, so feel free to take your time, but it might be easier to just tell me."

Alex downs the rest of his drink and pushes his glass forward toward me. "Get me another just like that and I'll tell you."

I mix him another Jack and Coke and set it down in front of him, ready to hear what's wrong with my best friend tonight. "There you go. Not too much soda. So what's the problem?"

After he takes a gulp, he lets out a heavy sigh. "It's Hailey's friend Meadow. I think we could have a good time, if I could ever get her to stick around for more than a half hour. She had to rush off back to work tonight. That's the third time in a row. Well, second if you aren't counting her not even sticking around here that night we were supposed to meet."

His moping and why he's so upset make me laugh. "So you have a hard time with a fellow workaholic. I'm guessing you don't appreciate the irony in all of this. Too bad because it's rich."

Alex twists his expression, shaking his head. "I'm not a workaholic. I have no idea why you think that. I don't work because there's a ton of shit to get done. I enjoy my work. I love my work. That's not the same as a workaholic," he protests before taking another drink.

"Probably wouldn't have worked out anyway. She gorgeous and all, but I doubt she's a freak like you."

I know that will get him going. He's not exactly a freak. What he likes isn't necessarily any different than most guys. What makes Alex different is the intensity of how he likes the run-of-the-mill things.

He's a pure hedonist, through and through.

"So enjoying life is being a freak? Maybe I should

be a surly bastard who goes around being miserable and picking fights with people?"

I smile at his swipe at my own recent behavior. "Sounds like you're doing just that right now."

As he tilts his glass up to his mouth, he grins at me. "You know, you're lucky to be with someone like Hailey. She was working on doing something with strawberries that sounded incredible. Maybe I should change my policy of dating women in my business."

"Go find your own beautiful baker. Hailey's taken."

He looks down the bar and then up at me. "So what are you doing here on a Monday when you could be with her?"

"Filling in for Katelyn," I answer, practically grunting my disgust. "First her sister nearly makes me lose my girlfriend when she pulls that shit at the anniversary party, and now she's out until Thursday. I thought Wilder was a huge cock block. He's got nothing on the twins."

After he finishes his drink, Alex sets his glass down on the bar and frowns. "You should have heard him after you left the other day. To hear him talk, it was all your fault."

"What? Him busting in when I'm trying to be alone with Hailey out at the house or the fight? In my opinion, both were his fault."

"No, the problem between you two. He was acting like he has no idea why you're not his biggest fan."

I roll my eyes at the thought of any excuse Wilder could come up with. "Well, I'm not even sure he has a problem with me. I mean, other than the general problem he seems to have with everyone in the world. That whole miserable fuck who hates all of humanity thing is such bullshit, but I don't know if he has a problem with me. I know I have a problem with him, and his showing up with those two shitheads the other night didn't make it any better."

"Is that why you were acting weird with Hailey when you talked to her? She asked me about it, but I sidestepped giving her an answer since I had no idea. I think she's worried, though."

Hearing Hailey told Alex something was wrong between us irritates me. "Why would she say that?"

He gives me a look like I just asked the dumbest question in the world. "Because she's worried."

"Well, she has no reason to be. I was just pissed that I had to work so many nights this week. That's all."

"Don't tell me. Tell her."

"What else could she think was wrong?" I ask, once more getting pissed off that I have to be here tonight.

Alex shrugs, but I see in his expression he thinks there could be something else. "I don't know. Maybe she's gets worried when someone acts like they're a hundred percent about her and then gets all moody. That running hot and cold thing you do isn't easy if you aren't used to it like I am, and that's only because I've known you all my life. She hasn't, Cade. It's not surprising she might get uneasy."

I nod, but I know it's more than just that. True, I

do tend to run hot and cold like he said, but for Hailey, I know she's got to be wondering if the same thing that happened with that asshole who cheated on her is happening again.

Damn Katelyn and whatever crisis she's dealing with this week. She and her sister should get together with my goddamned cousin. They could be the cockblock triplets. Somebody should make up T-shirts they can wear so people know to steer clear of all three of them.

"So, are you planning on giving up on Hailey's friend? I don't think two people who love to work are a good fit," I say, teasing Alex once again.

"We'll see. She might be just like me. You never know."

The wicked look in his eyes tells me he hopes Meadow is just like him. She seemed pretty normal to me, though. No weird wearing of cartoon costumes as an everyday way to dress. No bizarre habits like most of Alex's girlfriends. Not exactly the usual type of woman he likes to pursue.

"If all she does is work, you might never know either."

"Fuck you. I don't know why I even talk to you," he snaps before pushing his glass toward me.

"Because I'm your best friend. Are you that drunk that you forgot?" I ask with a laugh.

"Fuck you. I'm going home. You around tomorrow? I'm working early, so I'll be off by nighttime."

I shake my head as I spread my arms. "All of this is what I get until Thursday. Then I'll get to see Hailey."

"That sucks. Too bad you don't have a trust fund or something that would allow you to just relax and enjoy life," Alex says, throwing his head back and laughing. When he finishes, he smiles. "That's for busting my balls about Meadow. Now we're even."

"No, now it's my turn to say fuck you. Stop over Wednesday afternoon, if you aren't busy chopping every carrot in the known world. We can go out on the water for a few hours before I have to put the ball and chain on and come back here."

Alex slaps me on the shoulder. "Will do. Have a good one."

And with that, the most interesting part of my workday walks out, leaving me with a handful of customers in need of more booze. Too bad I don't have one of those handy, dandy trust funds.

CHAPTER THIRTEEN

$\mathcal{H}$ailey

EVEN THOUGH CADE AND I TALKED EVERY DAY AND he made sure to explain that nothing was wrong on Tuesday when he called, Thursday night couldn't come fast enough for me. After all my experimenting, I have five desserts I love and hope will wow Brooke Dunning on Friday.

Except for the fact that I haven't heard from her yet, and it's already four o'clock on the day before.

Did she change her mind? Or maybe she decided the apple tarts she had last week really weren't that good. They could have been better. I went a little too heavy with the cinnamon. Or maybe she doesn't want to do extra spin classes. I couldn't blame her for that. Just the thought of them makes me grimace in pain.

All of this races through my head as I wait for

Cade to return from the kitchen with a drink. By the time he walks into the living room, my panicked thoughts have made my stomach twist into knots and my mouth feels like someone has sucked all the moisture out, leaving nothing but a dried up husk for my tongue.

Definitely not the way I wanted our first night together all week to go.

"You look like something's wrong. What happened in the time between me going to get you a drink and now?" he asks as he sits down next to me on the couch and sets my glass on the coffee table in front of us.

"Nothing. Just my normal worrying. I still haven't heard from Brooke Dunning. Do you think she changed her mind?" I ask and then lean forward to grab my drink.

The cool water feels so good when it hits my tongue, and I hope it does wonders for my upset stomach. What would help is if I wouldn't get stressed out over this.

"No, I don't think she changed her mind," Cade says with a sweet smile. "I bet she's just been busy."

I don't know if I believe that, but it doesn't matter. The more I keep thinking about tomorrow, the more freaked out I get. Either she's forgotten or changed her mind, which would make me feel terrible, or everything's fine and I'll hear from her tonight about what time to go to her hotel tomorrow, which will make me feel even more nervous.

"Tonight might not have been a good idea. I don't think I'm going to be very good company."

Talk about an understatement.

"No way. I have something good planned, and you watch. You're going to love it and be so relaxed that you'll stop worrying about tomorrow. Just sit back and unwind. Tonight is all about you."

Cade's trying to be helpful, but I'm worried if all the focus is on me tonight, then I'll have nothing to occupy my mind and I'll keep stressing out about this thing with Brooke. What I need is to focus my mind on something else entirely.

"I think it might be better if it was all about you, to be honest. Then I'd be able to get my mind off what's troubling me," I confess, hoping I'm not ruining his plans.

His mouth turns up in a wicked smile that makes him look so incredibly sexy. "Well, that could work too with what I have planned."

Cade slides his hand up my thigh and leans in to kiss me. "We can take turns, or the first part of the night can be all about you and then the next part can be all about me. Whatever you like. It's your call."

As his fingers slowly creep up my leg, I feel the familiar ache I've carried with me all week since I was with him last. "Did you plan to just have sex all night?"

He stops his hand and looks up at me, all worried. "Sort of. We could do something else too, though. Whatever you want."

The way he says that sounds so sincere and almost innocent that I giggle. I don't have a problem with him wanting to spend all night in bed. The last thing I want to do is go out tonight and be around people when I've missed him so much all week.

"I'm not really hungry right now. Not for food, anyway. And I don't really want to go out."

His smile returns, lighting up his dark eyes. "Good. So do we focus on you first or me?"

"Your choice."

Gently, he pushes me back on the couch and settles in between my legs. Looking up, he watches me as he pushes my sundress up over my hips and then inches my panties down.

"This was all I could think about last night. Just lay back and let me give you something good to take your mind off everything."

He tosses my underwear behind him and pushes my legs open, his palms pressing my thighs out so I'm completely exposed to him. That ache in my belly I've had all week grows stronger now, and I can barely wait to feel his mouth on me.

Cade stops just before his mouth touches my pussy, and his warm breath teases what's about to happen. Desperate for his tongue to flick against my excited skin, I lift my hips, but he pushes me back down onto the couch.

"Somebody can't wait. I love it," he whispers so close to my pussy that each word thrills me.

"Please…" I murmur, unable to get more than just that word out as every bit of my brain focuses on the moment when he'll finally touch me.

Instead of pressing that beautiful mouth of his to me, he runs his fingertip up my wet slit until he reaches my clit. "Patience. I'm supposed to be taking your mind off your worries."

I look down at him and smile. "Trust me. You are. Now all I can think about is how much I want you to use that perfect tongue to get me off."

"Since it's your turn first, your wish is my command, my lady," he says as he stares up at me with those dark brown eyes so sensual and mischievous.

And then I finally feel what I've waited for, and it's like heaven.

His tongue drags over my delicate skin, exciting every inch it touches on its way to the bundle of nerves needy for attention, and when he flicks the tip of his tongue against it, my eyes roll back in my head it feels so damn good. Cade gently sucks my clit into his mouth and presses his fingertips into my thighs, marking the flesh so I'll probably have faint bruises for days to remind me of how much I enjoyed this.

He lets out a tiny, satisfied hum against me that races straight to the center of my being. Arching my back, I press my pussy to his mouth, dying for all he can give me. He devours it, like a famished man with his favorite food after too long denied it. I stuff my hands into his dark hair and hold him to me as I rock my hips back and forth.

Cade rides each movement of my body, his hands holding me tightly enough that he controls every part of this for me, even if he lets me move to feel as much as I can. I whimper with each lap of his tongue up my slit and cry out softly when he sucks my clit between his lips. He sets a tempo each time — slow up and then suck. Over and over, and I wait for each part to follow the other.

Just when I think I can't take another moment of the sweet agony, he changes things up. Sliding a finger inside me, he begins to fuck me, hooking his fingertip just right so it touches that spot that makes hints of colors shatter behind my eyes. When he slides a second finger in and sucks my clit into his mouth, that's all it takes. What look like fireworks explode in my closed eyes, and I moan loudly enough that his neighbors have to be able to hear.

"Oh, God! Yes...yes...right there. God, don't stop..." I beg, and Cade's happy to keep giving me every last lick I need.

When the last tremor of my release finally subsides, he lifts his head and licks his lips. His mouth shines with my juices, and he gives me a satisfied grin like he's the one who just got off.

"That's a nice start to the night, don't you think?" he asks as he sits back on his heels looking like a conqueror who's taken some prized territory for his own.

"Definitely," I say in a dreamy voice.

I can't seem to put together a full sentence to tell him how utterly incredible he just made me feel. Stretching my legs, I feel a phantom quake from my orgasm, and I press my thighs together to make it last.

"I fucking love how you are when I do that," Cade says.

Hovering over me, he leans down and gently kisses my lips. I taste myself on them and run my tongue along my bottom lip. "I love how you do that, so it works out well."

He sits down on the couch at my feet and unzips his pants to take his cock out. Already rock hard, it stands up straight, and he gives it a few tugs before turning to look over at me with pure need in his eyes.

"Change of plans. I want that beautiful mouth on me. Now."

Cade pushes the coffee table back with his foot, making way for me to sit in front of him. I think about straddling his hips and moving things along to the next phase of the night for a moment, but I lower to my knees instead. He wants me to suck his cock, and after the release he just gave me, I'd say yes to anything the man asked at this moment.

I wrap my fingers around the base while he opens his pants to give me all the room I need. He didn't wear any underwear tonight, a sign he had planned for us to spend all night in bed. No matter. They'd just get in the way now.

My gaze locked on his, I give the underside of his cock a long lick from balls to head. His eyes go cloudy and even darker, if that's possible, like just the simple act of my tongue on his flesh changes him.

His silky soft skin tastes faintly salty, and when I take the head into my mouth, that flavor increases. He's large and forces my jaw to open more so I feel a twinge of pain, but I push it away. I want to make him feel like he just did for me.

Cade lets out a throaty moan and stuffs his hand into my hair, tightening his fingers in the strands so tiny licks of pain dance across my scalp. It's something that excites me instead of hurting me, and I respond by slowly lowering my head to take more of him into my mouth.

He's patient for a minute or so as I gradually ease his cock inside me, but that tolerance gives out about halfway down and his hand pushes me the rest of the way. He bumps up against the back of my throat, and I can't stop myself from gagging and moving away from him.

Above me, he says in a faraway voice, "Take all of it, baby. Let me see you take all of it."

God, he's so sensual that I want to do just that, so I relax and ease every last inch of his cock inside my mouth until the head touches the back of my throat again. This time, I don't gag, and he lets out a passionate moan that sounds like it comes from the depths of his soul.

"Fuck, Hailey. That feels so good. Don't stop."

I slide my mouth up his shaft and then dip down again, this time faster and harder so I slam down on him. Looking up at him, I see him watching me with rapt attention, like my sucking his cock is all he's ever wanted to see in his life.

Scratching my fingernails over the skin between his hips, I bob my head up and down, finding a rhythm that excites me. If he touched between my legs, Cade would find me drenched. I want to make him come like he did for me, and just the thought that I can thrills me so I run wet.

His hold on my hair tightens a minute later, and I

sense he's getting close. He pushes my head down on him, groaning softly when I swipe my tongue over his balls when I reach the base of his cock. When I think he might be just seconds away from coming, I suck harder, my heart slamming in my chest, and a moment later, he floods my mouth with everything he has.

After he finishes, I sit back and smile up at him. He looks down at me through half-lidded eyes, so utterly sexy and satisfied that I have to stop myself from going down on him again.

"Fuck. I'm not sure I can move now," he says with a smile.

I slide my hands up his thighs and take a deep breath, ready to climb on top of him and feel him fill me up. "No need for you to move."

Straddling his hips, I kiss him on the mouth and whisper against his lips, "You have no idea how excited that got me."

Cade cups my ass and squeezes, dragging my pussy the full length of his cock. "I think I do," he says with a chuckle.

CHAPTER FOURTEEN

ade

DAMN, SHE'S SO FUCKING WET AGAINST ME THAT MY strength suddenly comes roaring back. A minute ago, I wasn't sure my legs would even work, but knowing how much sucking my cock excited her has given me a second wind I thought I'd have to wait at least a few minutes for.

But I don't want to just sit here and watch Hailey ride me tonight. No, this night is about taking her mind off everything but us, so it calls for something more.

I lift the bottom of her dress and say, "Time for this to come off."

Hailey gives me a confused look but raises her arms to help me slip the dress over her head.

Underneath, she's naked, which is perfect for what I want to do next.

After I give her nipples a suck and pull her mouth down to mine to kiss her long and deep, I give her a little tap on the ass. "Up and onto the couch."

That gets me yet another confused look, but she doesn't ask what I have planned and stands up off me. I watch her sit down where I'd just been and shake my head.

"Turn around and on your knees. Hold onto the back of the couch," I say with a wink.

"Oh. Okay."

She does as I order, and I give my cock a few hard tugs looking at how beautiful she looks bent over and waiting for me to fuck her from behind. Leaning down, I press a tiny kiss to the middle of her back and make my way down to the base of her spine. Hailey arches her back with each kiss, a sign she's as eager as I am to get down to business.

I grip the base of my cock and aim it for her cunt while my other hand grabs her hair and pulls her head back. With one hard thrust, I bury myself in her and say low in her ear, "Ready?"

She whimpers her answer, and I pull out of her so just the head is still inside. Then I push my hips forward and fill her completely again as I tighten my hold in her hair.

Her cunt is wet and perfect around my cock. "That's it. This feels so fucking good."

Hailey says something, but I can't understand because her mouth is pressed against a cushion. I begin fucking her in earnest, watching how beautiful her body looks when my cock disappears into her perfect cunt. Her hands grip the back of the couch until her knuckles turn white, but she doesn't want me to stop any more than I want to.

I sink my fingers into her hips and fuck her hard, loving how she reacts. Hailey moans, and I swear my cock swells inside her so her body grips me tightly. It's like she was made for me and only me, and I can't get enough of her.

"Cade, I'm slipping.." she says, and I look down to see her knees coming off the couch.

"Don't worry. I got you."

Hooking my arm under her stomach, I lift her and move her forward so she's back on the cushion. She turns to look back and me, and I see her teeth sink into her bottom lip. Fuck, she looks sexier than I think I can handle.

A few strokes more into her and I feel her cunt tighten around me. Her hands curl into tight fists, and she lowers her head so the angle changes for us. This position feels even better, and a second later, she screams my name as she comes hard on my cock.

It only takes a few more thrusts and I'm right there with her as her body milks me to release. I rear back and sink into her one last time before it feels like the top of my head is going to blow off. I see her press her palms against the back of the couch to push back against me, and then I'm lost.

I collapse on top of her and we both fall to the couch, exhausted and satisfied out of our minds.

Breathless, she and I search for air, panting after the best sex I've ever had.

"You okay under there? I'm not crushing you, am I?" I whisper in her ear and then kiss her neck softly.

She turns her head and through a curtain of hair, I see her smile. "This time, I definitely can't walk. I think I'm boneless."

I don't know why, but all I can think of when she says that is chicken. Chuckling, I kiss her again. "That was incredible."

As I sit up, she rolls over and looks at me oddly. "Then why are you laughing?"

She's so beautiful lying there that I hesitate to ruin the mood with something stupid, but I tell her the truth. "Because when you said you were boneless, I thought of chicken."

Hailey's expression twists into one of disbelief, but then she sits up and laughs. "Super hot sex makes you think of chicken? Thank God you have a big dick or I'd have to think twice about sleeping with you again."

"Well, thank God for small favors."

Leaning over, she kisses me. "Big favors, honey. Big favors."

As we sit there after incredible sex, in each other's arms while we try to catch our breath, I think about how many women I could never have that conversation with. They'd take it personally or think it was dumb. They might even get their feelings hurt by my laughing and not accept anything I say after that.

Hailey's different, though. Different from every other woman I've ever known. I like being able to laugh with her while we're lying naked next to one another.

"Why so quiet? Thinking about getting something to eat? Boneless wings, maybe?" she asks with a cute little giggle.

I pull her to me and smile at how comfortable it feels to be with her. "Actually, I was just thinking that I like that we can be this way together."

"Silly?" she asks as she nuzzles the space between my jaw and my shoulder.

"Real. I don't have to lie to you, even when my brain thinks of something stupid, probably because of a lack of oxygen after a round of great sex. I like that about us."

Looking up at me, she nods. "I like that too."

We sit there in silence recovering and after a little while, Hailey taps her finger against my arm. "Did you fall asleep?"

I squeeze her to me, loving how this feels more natural than anything else in my life. "No. Just recharging after that round."

Before she can say anything else, her phone buzzes in her purse on the floor. Grabbing it, she holds it up in front of us. "I need to get this in case it's Brooke telling me what time tomorrow. Sorry."

On the screen, I read that Brooke Dunning wants her to come to the Regent Hotel at one o'clock tomorrow. Room 544.

Hailey points at her phone and smiles like an excited little kid. "I thought maybe she had changed her mind. This is so great!"

"It is. You're going to be great tomorrow."

She tosses her phone back into her purse and sits up next to me. Her smile is gone, replaced by a far too serious look for someone who's just gotten such good news.

"What's wrong?" I ask, unsure what could be making her so unhappy.

Looking down at her hands, she says, "Would you come with me? I know it's an imposition, but it would be so great to have you there for moral support in case it turns out I'm terrible at podcasts."

I lift her chin and give her my answer. "It's not an imposition. If you want me there, I'm there. And I don't think you're going to be terrible at podcasts. Don't you just have to talk?"

"What if my mind goes blank or I stammer a lot when she asks me questions?"

The fear in her eyes is real, so I pull her to me and press a kiss to the top of her head. "You're going to be fantastic. You're a great chef and great at sex and the best girlfriend in the world, so of course you're going to be terrific at this too."

Tilting her head back, she looks up at me. "You're going to give me a big head."

"Good. Some people should have big heads. I believe in you, Hailey."

She takes a deep breath and lets it out slowly. "Thank you. And thank you for agreeing to come with me tomorrow. Just knowing you're nearby will keep me calm."

The idea that I could do that for anyone shocks me

more than it would anyone else, I imagine. The guy who runs hot and cold and can't get his life together keeps this incredible woman calm.

I'd be crazy to ever let her go just for that reason alone. But there are a million others too, and I silently promise never to forget any single one of them.

CHAPTER FIFTEEN

$\mathcal{H}$ailey

MY ARMS FULL OF THE DESSERTS TO TAKE TO Brooke Dunning's hotel room, I look into the backseat of Cade's car and then back at him. "Maybe we should take my car. I don't want to ruin yours if anything spills."

He takes the top tray out of my hands and moves toward the rear of the car. "If anything spills, I'll get it detailed. You'll owe me one night of mind-blowing sex. We can put it all in the trunk and everything will be fine."

I blush at his mention of sex knowing my parents are just inside the restaurant and follow him to the back of the car. He helps me load the trays and pans and then stops to kiss me.

"I might just swerve a few times so I get that night of sex."

"Please don't. I'll deliver on the sex no matter what. I promise."

Cade laughs at me, and I sense I took him too seriously there. "I wouldn't do that. I know you need these to look as good as they taste. Presentation is everything, right?"

"Yes, and I'm sorry I'm so literal right now. I'm just a little nervous."

"No worries," he says before kissing me again. "Now let's get going. I promise to drive the speed limit for the first time in my life too."

"Okay. Let me run in and tell my parents goodbye. I'll be right back."

Busier than usual, the kitchen feels crowded now as I run in to see my mom and dad. They pretend to be busy, but I know by the way they're just standing near my station that they've been talking instead of working.

"We're going to leave now. Wish me luck!"

My mother, always the more emotional parent, opens her arms and pulls me in for a big hug. "Oh, honey. This is so exciting! Have a good time, okay?"

When she leans away from me, still holding my shoulders, though, I see hope in her eyes. While she doesn't talk about it every day, she can't escape the truth of how the restaurant is faring lately.

If only Brooke Dunning could get more people to come in because they heard about my desserts on this podcast, business would pick up. I know it would.

"I will, Mom," I say with a smile.

My father stands stoically off to the side, as if none of this podcast nonsense interests him in the least. His arms folded across his chest, he looks like he's doing his best statue impression. I know the truth, though. He may not be as hopeful as my mother that today will turn things around for Comfort Food, but he's wished something would.

I so want today to be that something.

"Will we be able to listen to this podcast thing at some point?" he asks in a serious tone.

"Yes, Dad. I don't know when, but I'll find out."

"Don't talk too fast. I swear to God every time I turn on the radio or TV, people are talking too fast. They sound like squawking chickens running around with their heads cut off."

I stare at him for a moment, not sure how a chicken without a head could make any noise. "Okay. No squawking Hailey. Got it. I have to go. I don't want to be late."

For the first time in this conversation, he finally cracks a smile as he opens his arms to hug me. "Enjoy yourself, honey. You deserve this."

"Thanks, Dad. I will."

With a kiss for both of them, I hurry back through the kitchen past well-wishes from the cooks and servers out to the car where Cade waits for me. When I jump in and we take off much slower than he usually drives, I look over at him and smile.

"Thanks for toning down the speed today."

"No problem. What did your parents have to say?"

All I can think of is my father's chicken comment. "To have a good time and don't sound like a chicken with her head cut off."

Cade switches lanes and then turns to look at me with confusion written all over his face. "Is this an inside joke in your family? How would a chicken sound without a head? Do they mean make sure not to lose your voice? I don't get it."

With a shrug, I laugh. I don't explain it to him since it's silly anyway.

THE REGENT HOTEL SITS DOWN ON THE waterfront, prime real estate in the city, and from the moment we drive into the parking garage, I sense this is very different from what I'm used to. By the time we get off the elevator on the fifth floor, I start to doubt this is something I should be doing.

"This place is nice," Cade says casually as we walk toward Room 544. "A little on the stuffy side for my tastes, but nice."

I turn to look at him in shock that he's describing this hotel as merely nice. "Did you see the fountain in the lobby? That thing goes two floors high. And all the decorations looked like gold. Not painted gold but real gold."

"Yeah, but they could have put some TVs in the lobby where all that water was. It's nice, though, I guess."

I suspect Cade is more nonchalant about the fancy style of the Regent Hotel than I am because he comes from money. To me, this place is stunning. It's the kind of hotel you see in movies when royalty have to sleep away from their castles.

He stops and points at one of the white hotel room doors. "544. Looks like we're here. Ready?"

Shaking my head, I admit the absolute truth of what I feel at this moment. "No. I'm shaking like a leaf, and my stomach feels like it's about to push out everything I've eaten this morning."

As always, he smiles and leans in to kiss me softly on the lips, his dark eyes filled with kindness he probably thinks I need so I don't unravel like a cheap suit right here in the hallway on the fifth floor of the ultra-fancy Regent Hotel. "You're going to be great. I can't wait to see you wow her with these desserts. I want you to know that after we're done I plan to eat one of those whoopie pies, so she better not block out a week of extra spin class to gobble the last one down."

"I love you. You know that?" I say, trying to find some calm inside my terrified brain.

"I do, and I love you too. So let's go in there and do some podcasting. There's a whoopie pie with my name on it, and I can practically hear it calling to me right now. If we don't get in there, I'm going to have to rescue it, so we better get this show started before I do."

His sexy smile and silly joke bring me some relief from the stress building inside me, and I knock on the door to get this day underway. Everything will be okay. What's the worst that can happen? All the desserts are terrible, she announces that to the entire world, and I go back to my parents to apologize and swear I'll learn how to waitress better than anyone ever has before to help them save on at least one salary.

As I watch for the door to open, I silently pray to God none of that happens as memories of my one and only stint as a server run through my head. I was so terrible. I tried it one summer in high school. I had a tendency to drop trays full of food, sometimes in customers' laps.

Please don't make me have to go back to that again. Nobody wants that. Really.

The door finally opens, and a tall brunette with the longest neck I've ever seen on a person is standing there. That one feature steals all my attention from her beautiful face, and I have to force myself to look up at her lovely hazel eyes and only them.

"Hello! You must be Hailey. Please come in. Brooke is waiting for you," she says in a chipper voice before stepping back to let Cade and me into the room.

As I imagined while we walked through the hotel, the room is gorgeous. Rooms is technically the correct description. We walk into what looks like a living room that's bigger than the apartment I had in college. Two white couches with tiny pink flowers face one another, one on each wall, and in between sits an enormous coffee table. The room is so big that none of these pieces of furniture make walking through the room toward a large dining table in front of a bank of windows on the far wall difficult at all.

Definitely bigger than my entire apartment.

Brooke sits at the table near the windows and practically jumps up out of her chair when we walk in. Dressed in white pants and a red shirt, she looks stunning.

"I am so glad to see you again, Hailey. You can just put everything in your hands on the coffee table. We'll be talking over at that table over there. I see you brought a guest."

I nod and hurry to introduce everyone. "Brooke, this is Cade. My boyfriend. He came to help with all the trays since I'd never be able to get these all up here. Cade, this is Brooke Dunning, a food blogger who has a national podcast."

Brooke quickly adds, "And Hailey and Cade, please meet my assistant Tabitha. She'll be helping today."

We all shake hands and smile before Cade and I set the desserts on the coffee table and I begin to arrange them. Nervous, I nearly knock over the container of pink and green macarons to send them spilling all over the floor. Thankfully, Cade catches it and sets it down on the table.

Taking my hands in his, he whispers in my ear, "It's okay. This is going to be great, right?"

I nod and take a deep breath in. This is going to be great. I've made the best desserts I can, and Brooke's going to love them.

"Your boyfriend is so nice, Hailey. My ex-husband would have just let those cookies fly everywhere and then he wouldn't have helped to clean them up either," Brooke says and then laughs.

"I'm just a little nervous. Thank God, Cade never gets nervous. He's always calm, cool, and collected."

She and Tabitha look over at him and smile. "See, that's what I like to see in a man. Cool. It's a very sexy trait but so many men just can't pull it off," Brooke says, still staring at him as her assistant turns her focus to the desserts now arranged on the coffee table.

"Brooke, look at how gorgeous all of these are!" Tabitha coos, pointing down at the white chocolate torte topped with chocolate morsels and plump raspberries. "Is that white chocolate? Did Brooke tell you that's one of our favorites?"

I smile and quietly let out a sigh of relief at my choice of that dessert for today. "It is, and I think you're going to love it. It's one of my favorites too."

"I'm going to need a month of spin classes after this, but it will all be worth it," Brooke gushes as she heads toward the desserts. "I think we should taste some now before we get started. Tell me about every one and why you made it."

Turning to face Cade, I give him a panicked look. I had planned on talking about all of that during the podcast. If I explain things now, what will I say then? He simply nods and smiles, like he knows I'm unraveling but he's here and everything's going to be okay.

"Well, I thought I'd tell that in the podcast. I don't want to bore you with telling it twice."

Brooke waves off my worry and grabs a macaroon.

"Oh, don't worry about that. You can tell me then, if you like that better. Just make sure you give my listeners a full story. They're used to that after reading my recipes on my website."

My father's criticism of that very trait of food bloggers flashes through my mind, and I can't help but smile. He'd have a lot to say right now about that and so many other things. Hopefully, I can channel him when it comes time for the podcast.

"This chocolate creation is divine!" Tabitha squeals before taking her second bite of Boston Cream Whoopie Pie. "Brooke, this is to die for. I'm serious. Try this!"

I glance over at Cade and see him giving me a fake scowl, like he's not happy these two women are so focused on the dessert he wants to eat in a little while. I give him a smile and silently promise to make him his own special whoopie pie if it turns out there are none left when we leave today.

After they try each dessert, leaving a single whoopie pie for me to take home for Cade, Brooke pats her nonexistent belly like it's some huge thing and motions for me to follow her. "Time to get this thing going. I have to tell you, I think I'm in love with every single dessert, but that Boston Cream pie creation is just heavenly. Do you mind leaving that last one for me when you go? It's just so good."

Out of the corner of my eye, I see Cade smile. "Oh, that would be no problem. I'm going to make a special batch of them for Cade when I get home because he loves them too."

Brooke's eyes light up, and she looks past me toward where he's sitting on one of the couches. "He obviously has good taste. And not just in desserts. You two make such a darling couple. I love it!"

I thank her for being so sweet, and as we begin to actually talk about the desserts and me, I find I have a lot to say about many topics. Whatever fear I had before I sat down in front of her at that table evaporates, leaving me to have fun talking about why I love to bake and my parents' restaurant.

And my father won't be disappointed since I didn't talk too fast and I didn't bury all the good information about Comfort Food beneath a ton of words and some long-winded story about my childhood like food bloggers generally do.

By the time we finish, an hour has passed and I'm so excited I could talk for another sixty minutes. Brooke finishes what she calls goodies for the production crew, which seems to mean repeating something about what we talked about and who we are, and turns to me with a big smile that I hope means this was a success.

"Hailey, that was so much fun. I only have one question to ask you. Where do I find a yummy man like the one you have? He doesn't happen to have any brothers, does he?"

For a second, I wonder if she's just being nice, but the intensity in her eyes while she waits for me to answer her question tells me she's serious. "He just happened to walk into the restaurant one day. We sort of stumbled onto one another. To be honest, considering that he works at a nightclub and I rarely go out, especially to clubs, I doubt we'd ever meet. He doesn't have any brothers, but he's got a family full of cousins. One of them, Alex, looks a lot like him and is a chef at CK."

Her mouth drops open like this is the best news she's heard all day. "Really? I might have to go there before I leave town. So Cade works at a nightclub? Which one? What does he do?"

"Club X. He's a bartender there," I proudly tell her.

"A bartender and a baker. It's a perfect pairing. Thank you so much for coming here and talking to me and my listeners today. I hope your family's restaurant gets a ton of traffic because of it. It's a charming place I know so many people would love."

I have to stop myself from crying I'm so relieved at this moment. Brooke Dunning, a major food blogger with millions of fans, loves my work and had fun talking to me, a nobody when it comes to cooking.

"Thank you so much, Brooke. You've been so wonderful. I can't tell you how much I appreciate this."

When Cade and I get out into the hallway, I throw my arms around his neck and jump up and down I'm so happy. "She loved it all! I had so much fun. Did it sound okay? I think it sounded okay. I made sure to mention Comfort Food a bunch of times, and I didn't sound like a total idiot when I told the stories about why I love blueberry and lemon desserts and how chocolate should be a major food group. That didn't sound stupid, did it?"

Always the calm one, he smiles and presses a kiss to my forehead. "You were as great as I thought you would be. That's going to be her most interesting episode, I bet. I'm so proud of you, Hailey."

There isn't a happier person in the world than me right now.

CHAPTER SIXTEEN

ade

AFTER CELEBRATING HAILEY'S SUCCESSFUL DEBUT as a podcast star with her parents at Comfort Food, I have to drag myself away to get to work. Standing behind the main bar at Club X is the last place I want to be tonight. I don't have a choice, though. That's the worst part of it. No choice.

I intentionally miss my father's overly enthusiastic team meeting to start off the night, unable to stomach that much gung-ho tonight. Slipping in as he busies himself with some drama on the upper floor, I take my position at the front bar and get to work making sure all the liquor we may need is available and the glasses necessary for the night are ready.

When I finish, I look around wondering where the rest of the staff is for the front bar tonight. He surely didn't schedule only me to run the main bar on a Friday. My father is a better businessman than that.

As I look around for anyone to find out who's supposed to be up here with me, the man himself walks down the stairs and sees me. "I wish you'd get here for the staff meetings. I had important things to tell everyone and you missed it all."

"Sorry. My cheerleading uniform is at the dry cleaners. I'm here, so you can tell me what I missed right now."

That snide crack gets me one of Stefan March's patented grimaces, sure to make any delicate person wither. Since I'm not sensitive and I've been on the receiving end of that look at least a million times in my life, I just shrug.

"You know I hate repeating myself. I swear you push my buttons intentionally, even though you know what the end result will be, Cade."

This is how our usual dance goes, but tonight, I'm not in the mood to fight with him. Today was great with Hailey, especially seeing her do so well with the podcast. I don't want to ruin that feeling by having yet another argument with my father.

So I do something I rarely try with him.

"I'm sorry, Dad. Today was a big day for my girlfriend, and I got caught up in that and ended up running late. What did I miss at the staff meeting?"

He takes a step back and stares at me like I've grown a second head out of my shoulder. At first, he doesn't seem to know what to say and looks around as if he needs someone to tell him that really just happened. I actually apologized.

Flustered, he takes a few moments to get his thoughts together since I'm sure he had this entire fight planned out in his head. Old habits die hard with us.

"Well, I decided I wanted to try something different tonight. The second floor ladies' room needs some repairs, but the plumber can't come until Monday. That means I need people to spend their time down here instead of upstairs. So I've rearranged some of the usual assignments. You'll be here with three people, not two. I put the twins at the back bar and brought Maya back up here. I know that isn't what you want, but I need you to give it your best, okay?"

Still expecting an argument from me, when he finishes talking, he takes a deep breath and lets it out on a heavy sigh. "It's only for one or two nights, but if you'd rather me put you somewhere else, I can do that."

"It's okay, Dad. Maya and I will do fine. Who's our third and fourth since you moved the twins to the back?"

"Antonio and Chelsea. They're getting fruit right now, so they'll be out soon."

"Okay. We'll be a little crowded, but we'll get the job done. Don't worry. I promise I won't douse Maya with the soda sprayer tonight," I say with a chuckle, remembering the time I shot her straight in the face with water after she dumped a beer over my head.

My agreeing with him throws my father off a little, and for a few seconds, he stands in front of the bar like he doesn't know what to do now. Not fighting with me appears to have sent his world off its axis.

"So, something happened with your girlfriend that was good? What was her big day about?" he asks in a low voice as he steps forward toward the bar.

Happy to tell this story for the second time today after I gave Alex all the details on my way over here, I explain, "She's a baker. She makes desserts for her family's restaurant, a little place called Comfort Food across town. A big food blogger heard about her after other bloggers began writing about the desserts, and today she had Hailey on her podcast to talk about what she makes. She did fantastic. I'm so proud of her. She's a little self-conscious about things because she didn't go to school for cooking like Alex. She actually went to school for psychology and was going for her master's, but things happened and that couldn't continue. So she started baking for her parents' restaurant and now this happened."

I suddenly cut my story short when I realize I've ventured into parts of Hailey's life I know she wouldn't want me talking about with anyone. My father smiles as I finish, giving me a nod like he approves.

"That sounds great. From what your uncles and Alex tell me, she must have a natural talent for baking if she didn't go to school because they rave about her desserts. I'm going to have to get myself over to that restaurant and try some so I'm not the only member of our family who hasn't sampled these delicious treats."

"She makes a Boston Cream Whoopie thing I hear is pretty incredible. I haven't gotten to try it yet, but the food lady raved about it."

"Sounds good. So you guys are doing okay?" he asks, hesitating as the words come out of his mouth.

I think about that and try to come up with the right way to describe how great things are between Hailey and me. We're more than okay. She makes me smile and happier than I've ever been in my life. That's a hell of a lot better than just okay.

But I still don't want to share her with my entire family yet, so I give him a noncommittal shrug and a vague answer. "We're good. It's still early, though. I guess I could fuck it up any time now."

He nods, like he agrees and turns to walk away. "Don't be so hard on yourself, Cade. You're a good man. I'm sure your girlfriend knows that."

Stunned those words came out of my father's mouth, I watch him walk away, surprised at how all that went with him. For one of the few times in my life, I didn't jump into a fight with him, and that ended up pretty good.

To hear him say he thinks I'm a good man makes this day for me. After seeing Hailey succeed with that food lady, this puts a cherry on top of a hell of a great afternoon.

. . .

FOR THE NEXT FOUR HOURS, I FEEL LIKE I'M walking on air. The club is packed with people, the music is pumping, and my fellow bartenders and I are making a killing on tips. Even Maya, the person who hates me most at Club X, seems in a good mood, so working with her turns out to be okay tonight.

Standing down at the far end of the bar closest to the door, I've got a few newly legal drinkers and their friends partying and paying more than usual customers do, so I give them some extra attention. I may not like this job, but I know how to do it damn well. Every tip I get I think about what gift I can buy Hailey to congratulate her on what she accomplished today.

Maybe a necklace or a bracelet? She doesn't seem to wear jewelry much, but that doesn't mean she wouldn't like some. Maybe a nice dinner out? That could be fun. Maybe we could go for a few nights down the coast to a secluded hotel that won't involve my cousin busting in with his idiot friends.

Someone tapping on my shoulder rips me out of my daydreams about Hailey's gift, and I turn my head to see Antonio in my face. Dark haired and literally the guy women come to see here at Club X, especially since he has a habit of sleeping with customers, sometimes two or three in a night, he points over his shoulder and smiles.

"Pretty lady down at the other end of the bar wants to talk to you," he says with a smile. "She asked for you by name."

Feeling like busting his ass, I say, "Not you? You must be losing your touch, man."

He screws his expression into one of disgust at my joking. "Don't you worry about my touch. It's all it's ever been."

I look down the bar to see a familiar face staring back at me — the food blogger woman. Brooke. Brooke what, though?

She waves me down to where she's standing, and as I slowly walk toward her, I try to remember her last name. Damnit. This is what I get for calling her the food lady so many times. Maybe it won't matter. It's not like we have to be formal and use last names in a bar.

"Cade March, boyfriend of the girl who makes those incredible desserts!" she squeals above the music.

Fuck. She remembers my last name. Great.

"You're a sight for sore eyes. Tabitha and I are spending our last night in Tampa and figured we should go out for a few drinks. I had no idea when I heard about Club X that it would be this crowded. We barely got in before security stopped the line," she says, thankfully moving on from names.

Glancing over her shoulder, I see her friend with the giraffe neck and smile. She's too far away to hear anything I might say, so I turn my focus back to Brooke standing at the bar.

"It's good to see you again. That was interesting today. The whole podcast thing, I mean. I know

Hailey had a great time. She talked about how much fun talking to you was all the way home."

Brooke excitedly waves her hand in between us, showing off some serious purple painted claws before she drops them to my forearm. I look down, unsure we're already at the touching one another stage, but I don't want to say anything and ruin things for Hailey. If this woman can help the woman I love, then I can handle her putting her hand on me. It's not like hundreds of other Club X customers won't do the same in the next few hours.

"It was so much fun! I hope it helps her. I'd love to help her in other ways too."

Seeing my chance to do something to make that happen, I lean forward and try to encourage her. "That would be great. I know if more people got to taste what she can make, they'd be lined up outside her parents' restaurant. You tried them, so you know what I mean."

She points at her ear and shakes her head before leaning toward me. "This music is really loud. Is there any place quieter we can talk? Do you get a break?"

I quickly scan the crowd in front of the bar and wave Antonio down to me. "It's not too busy, so I'm going to take ten. I'll be right in the office if things get hairy and you need me back ASAP."

My fellow bartender seems unfazed by my leaving and simply nods, so I come around the bar and point toward my father's office. "Come with me. It's quieter in there."

She smiles and latches onto my arm as I weave

through the crowd of people drinking and dancing. When we reach the office door, I open it and see my father isn't anywhere around.

Good. I don't want to talk to Brooke in front of him.

I guide her inside and shut the door, immediately drowning out all the noise from outside. Brooke takes a deep breath and looks around. It's not as impressive as her hotel room, but it will have to do.

"That's better," she says with a smile. "It really is loud out there. I don't know how you work in that night after night."

"Tonight's not even really bad," I say as I move her toward the couch over against the wall. "Sometimes it's loud enough that you wish you could wear earplugs, but then I'd never hear what anyone wants to drink. That would kill my tips, I think."

She laughs at my lame attempt at a joke, probably just being polite. I don't mind her thinking I'm stupid for that remark. I just want her to help Hailey.

"Whose office is this? Yours?"

"No. It's my father's. He owns the club. I merely work the bar."

The smile I get for that seems forced. "That's nice. You and your girlfriend work for your families' businesses."

Time to get her focused on how she can help Hailey.

"It's not really the same. I just bartend. Hailey actually creates things that her customers love. The first time I had her chocolate lace cookies, I knew they were special. Nothing I've ever mixed up tasted that good. I'd love it if more people could try them. They look like those little lace things grandmothers have around their houses and you think they're going to be light as air, but they're really creamy and very chocolatey."

"Tabitha loved the macarons. She said they were... what did she call them?"

When she can't seem to come up with the right word, I say, "Sweet?"

"Yes! That's it. I thought she said something else, but that was for that Boston Cream dessert. Tabitha said she thought it was sumptuous. Isn't that a wonderful word?" Brooke asks as she turns to face me on the couch.

"Sure. Sumptuous is a great word. I'd definitely say many of the desserts Hailey makes are sumptuous. The lighter ones might be better called tasty, but they're great too."

"I'm going to have to do a month's worth of spin classes after today. I couldn't help it, though. Those desserts seduced me into being bad."

My senses go on high alert as I listen to her talk and watch her hands move closer and closer to my thigh. Is she doing what I think she's doing?

"Is that how she got you, Cade? Did she seduce you with those tempting desserts?" Brooke asks as she nudges her leg against mine.

I know what's going on, and I need to make it very clear I'm with Hailey before this woman gets any ideas. I still hope I can get her to help Hailey more, but most important is she understands I'm all about my girlfriend. Period.

"She definitely did seduce me with them. I'm only human. One taste of her lace cookie and I was lost. What man could say no? That's why I think there's a great chance for anyone who wanted to help her get her treats out to the world."

As the last word leaves my lips, Brooke swings her leg over my lap, and a second later, she's straddling my hips. Before I can stop her, her lips cover mine in a heavy kiss and she jams her tongue halfway down my throat, moaning into my mouth.

Stunned, I push her away and shake my head. "Brooke, whoa. I'm with Hailey. She's my girlfriend. I just wanted to get you to help her. You need to get off me. Now."

I lift her by her waist and set her on her feet, hurrying to stand up before she jumps on my lap again but wondering if I can salvage anything to help Hailey. "It's okay. I mean, I'm flattered, but I'm with Hailey. Sorry."

She smooths the front of her pants and smiles like nothing just happened. "Can't blame a girl for trying. I still want to help her get the word out because I agree that people will like her desserts. No hard feelings?"

"No, no hard feelings," I say, relieved she didn't take my rejection and twist it to hurt Hailey.

"Well, time for me to go. Tabitha and I have an early flight tomorrow morning. Have a good night, Cade."

I watch her walk out as my father comes in and

hope I didn't ruin everything Hailey worked so hard at with her this afternoon. The problem is I don't think Brooke came here to talk about helping her with anything. What she wanted to do was help herself to me.

Fucking food lady.

My father walks by me on his way to his desk looking confused. "Who was that?"

"That food blogger from the podcast today."

He sits down and leans back in his chair, folding his arms behind his head. "Oh yeah? What did she want with you?"

"Nothing. I better get back behind the bar. Thanks for letting me use the office."

When I turn to leave, he laughs and says, "I don't recall you asking, but whatever. Hope it helped."

I just hope it didn't hurt.

CHAPTER SEVENTEEN

$\mathcal{H}$ailey

MY PHONE VIBRATES ACROSS THE DINING ROOM table, and I grab it to see who could be trying to talk to me at seven-thirty in the morning. I know it's not Cade since he didn't get home from the club until after three. His text telling me he loves me came in a three-eighteen, so it can't be him.

I vaguely recognize the number, but I answer it to hear Brooke already talking when I say hello. "We don't fly out until noon, so if you can get over here within the next half hour, I have some ideas for how to get the word out about those delicious treats of yours."

The next half hour? Thirty minutes? I'm still in the T-shirt and shorts I wore to bed last night, and I look like something the cat dragged in since I didn't remove my makeup before falling asleep!

But I can't miss an opportunity like this. Brooke might be able to help me get my desserts into the hands of someone who could write a great article about them and get even more people into the restaurant.

Jumping up from the table, I begin to dash around the house like a chicken with my head cut off. God, I really am my father's daughter!

"Okay, I'm getting ready right now. I'll be there in just a few minutes. Thank you so much, Brooke!" I say as I tear up the stairs to my bedroom.

"See you then!"

There's just enough time to wash my face and brush my teeth before I throw on a pair of capris and my favorite baby blue T-shirt with the word BELIEVE on it. Me without makeup isn't exactly the best, but when opportunity knocks, you have to answer the door no matter what you look like.

I drive like a maniac the whole way to the Regent Hotel, blowing through a red light a block away. With the sun shining in the bright blue sky, I didn't see it turn, but I doubt a cop would buy that story. I just hope no one saw me do that.

This time, I run through the hotel's lobby and barely notice anything as the furniture and decorations go by me in a blur on my way to the elevator. When the doors close and I press the button for five, I can finally catch my breath.

"This is going to be great. Just keep calm and try not to worry about not wearing makeup," I whisper into the elevator around me.

When I get to her room, I repeat that same idea and add, "You can do this. Remember you can do this."

"Hailey, it's so great you were able to come over so early today. Let's sit down and talk."

I immediately notice both Brooke and Tabitha have makeup on their faces. And they look incredible. Are those fake eyelashes they're wearing? God, my eyes must look like two pencil holes in a bedsheet compared to theirs.

Opening them as wide as I can get them, I nod and hope they don't pay too much attention to my face during this conversation. "I was so happy to hear from you today. Any help you can give me would be so appreciated."

Brooke waves her now purple tipped hands in front of her face, clearly excited about what she has to tell me this morning. "Well, I spoke to one of my fellow food bloggers, Jessie Tyson, and she wants to do a whole week of posts about you. She's local and has a really great audience, so I think it would give you a leg up you could use. She said to have you give her a call, so here's her number and all her info. Definitely check out her site. She gets tons of visitors every day."

She reaches across the space between us over the coffee table and hands me a sheet of note paper with all the details. "She said she hopes you'll call today, so I think she's excited too."

I clutch the paper like it has the secret to eternal life scrawled on it, thrilled for this assistance from a woman I just met last week. "Thank you so much, Brooke. This is so great of you."

She smiles, but it feels forced. Then she turns to look at Tabitha, who's never sat down, and I sense something's wrong. Did they have a fight? I had wondered if they were together and not just boss and assistant. Maybe I interrupted something when I got here so quickly.

"I have something I need to tell you, but I don't know how to say it."

My heart sinks. This is something about me. Something she doesn't know how to tell me. She doesn't think my desserts are good. She didn't like them. She was only pretending. But why did she call me over here this morning if she hated my stuff? Why would she recommend me to this Jessie woman too?

"Oh?"

That's all I can get out. Oh. Not even an oh my or an oh God. Just oh. Pretty much how my hopes being dashed to pieces sounds.

"This is so hard. I really like you, Hailey, and I think you're super sweet. I feel like in the short time we've known each other we've gotten to be like friends, and I would never let a friend be done wrong."

Now my stomach drops. "Done wrong?"

What does that mean?

She gives Tabitha another somber look and then falls silent. The seconds feel like hours as they tick by, and all I want to do is scream, "Who or what is doing me wrong and how do you know about this?"

Finally, she blurts out, "Your boyfriend. Cade? I don't think you can trust him."

Every word after his name hits me like a slap to the face, but somehow I get out, "What? Why can't I trust him? He's great."

For the first time, Tabitha speaks up as she walks over to take a seat on the couch next to Brooke. "You have no idea how much we don't want to tell you this. He seemed like such a great guy yesterday."

"He is a great guy," I say, my words trembling as they leave my mouth.

"No, he isn't," Brooke says quietly. "We saw him last night at that club he works at, and when I tried to talk to him, he was all over me. I couldn't believe it since he was so sweet with you when he was here."

"Cade wouldn't do that. He wouldn't do that to me."

"Tabitha was there. She witnessed it all."

All I can do is shake my head. They must be mistaken. Cade wouldn't do that. He just wouldn't.

"You must have him confused with someone else. Cade isn't like that."

The two women exchange looks, and then Brooke grabs her phone off the table. Holding it up, she turns it toward me and I expect her to show me a picture of Cade doing something. Instead, I hear voices coming from it, but I can't understand what they're saying.

"Who is that?" I ask, hoping against hope that it's not Cade's voice on that phone.

"I'm only human. What man could say no? I want you to get off."

Oh, God. He sounds so wrong. The guilt is coming through loud and clear. It's his voice. His words. Him hitting on Brooke.

It feels like someone has sucked all the air out of the room and I can't fill my lungs with a single breath to sustain me. Why would he do this? Was everything we've been to each other these past few weeks a lie?

My mind races as I struggle to fight back tears. Did he want to do that thing he did with that bartender the night I was at Club X? Was that all a lie he told me too?

"Hailey, I'm sorry I had to play that for you. You don't deserve that. You're so sweet and you're so talented. I just couldn't walk around with that on my conscience and not let you know the truth about him."

I shake my head but can't say a word, terrified if I utter a single syllable that I'll begin crying. I believed every word he said. Even when I had proof with my own eyes, I believed him.

Why would he do this to us? If he wanted someone else, why did he chase me like he did?

Through watery eyes, I look across at Brooke and know the truth. She's the type of woman he wants. She's gorgeous and successful and she probably comes from money.

Exactly the opposite of me.

"I better go, Brooke. Thanks for all your help."

"Okay. I hope I did the right thing, Hailey. I did, didn't I?" Brooke asks.

"Sure. Thanks. I have to go."

She says something as I hurry toward the door, but

I can't hear her over the sound of my heartbeat pounding in my ears. Nothing she could say now matters anyway.

By the time I get to my car, I can't stop the tears from coming anymore. I sit there in the parking lot of the expensive and luxurious Regent Hotel and sob like a baby, knowing I don't belong there just like I never belonged with Cade.

How could I have been so stupid?

CHAPTER EIGHTEEN

ade

ONE OF THE REASONS I HATE WORKING AT CLUB X so much is the hours. Getting home after three and not getting to sleep until four in the morning means I don't wake up until nearly noon and half the day is gone already. When it was just me, it didn't matter so much, but now that Hailey is in my life, having only a couple hours to see her before I have to go back to the club feels like a tradeoff I'm not willing to make.

I roll over and run my hand over the pillow she used the last time she slept in my bed. Pulling it to my face, I inhale deeply and smell the scent of that shampoo she uses. Vanilla? Or maybe coconut? I'm not sure. All I know is it reminds me of her.

Glancing at my phone through still-sleepy eyes, I see it's twelve-fifteen. Damn. I wanted to hang out with Hailey for a few hours before I need to be back at the club for seven.

My mind still groggy, I scrub the last of the night's sleep from my face and focus on the screen. Eleven messages. Who the fuck needed to talk to me that badly for the last eight hours that they left that many messages?

Even before I look, I'm guessing it's my father. He likes to send me an entire conversation in texts, each one two or three lines. I wake up thinking the world is on fire when it's just that he had an idea on some theme he thinks would work at the club and wants to know my opinion on it.

He's probably going to pitch that Y2K idea to me again. Dude, it wasn't good the first time you had it, so what would make you think a year later it's gotten any better? It's not a concept that's improving with age.

I set my phone back on the nightstand, not interested in dealing with that nonsense right after I wake up. That's really more of an in-person conversation anyway. Then I can shake my head when he says something really bizarre and hold my hand up to stop him before he gets too far into the crazy.

Staring up at the ceiling of my bedroom, I slowly come to life and wonder if I should read them. He's only going to continue messaging me if I don't. Then I'll have twenty or thirty to get through.

I reach my hand over and grab my phone, surrendering to the inevitability that I'll have to read them at some point. Better to get it over with now.

It only takes a split second to realize this isn't

another one-sided conversation from my father. They're all from Hailey. The first message hits me like a fist to the face, stunning me.

I never want to see you again. I know what you did, and there's no way you'll talk yourself out of this one. You must think I'm so stupid, but since I believed you with the girl on the bar, I bet you thought you'd fool me with this one too.

What does she mean? My eyes roam down the screen to the next one filled with even more hurt.

How could you do this to us? Why? And why Brooke? Was it to make sure it was as painful as possible for me?

My chest tightens with each word I read. Why does she think something happened with the food lady? Did she tell her? But nothing happened. Nothing at all.

I swing my legs off the side of the bed and walk out into the kitchen as I read the next message from Hailey.

Don't call me or come looking for me at the restaurant. I don't want to ever see you again.

Instead of reading any more, which will only show me how much she's hurting, I do exactly what she said not to and call her. I need to hear her voice. I need her to hear me tell her what really happened so she can know I never did anything with Brooke.

That I wouldn't blow up all we have together. Not with some lying food lady. Not with anyone.

That I love her and would never hurt her like that.

But her phone simply rings and rings with no

answer. I try again, but the same happens. And again and again for another four more times until the next time I try it goes directly to voicemail. I listen to her voice so sweet and bright when it says to leave her a message. I want to explain everything, but not in a voicemail message, for Christ's sake.

So instead I tell her the one thing that's truer now than it's ever been.

"Hailey, I love you. I'm coming over to see you, and I'm not leaving the restaurant until I talk to you. This is all a mistake, and I'm going to show you that. I love you."

I want to keep repeating that I love her so she can't think of anything else. Not whatever bullshit lie Brooke told her. Not whatever doubts she has because of what happened in her past. None of it. I just want her to know the one thing that's true is I love her.

She has to believe that.

HAILEY'S FATHER SEES ME AS I WALK IN THE FRONT door of Comfort Food, and I brace for what's likely to be the ugly scene that waits for me. I really don't want to have to fight through him to get to her, but I will today.

"Cade, good to see you!" he says as he walks over to greet me at the register. "Hailey's in the back. I'll go get her."

I quickly study his expression. It doesn't seem like he's being ironic or disingenuous in any way. Maybe he doesn't know?

"O—o—okay," I stammer out, unsure what's going on.

I read through all the messages before I got in my car and raced over here. Hailey never said she was mistaken or something had made her change her mind.

The double kitchen doors open, and she walks out looking as sweet and cheerful as usual. She doesn't smile so much as not frown, but when she stops in front of me, she points toward the door.

"I don't want to talk here. Let's go outside."

She doesn't sound furious or even sad. I don't understand.

By the time we get to the side of the restaurant out of sight, I'm totally confused. Her messages made it clear she's upset, but she's not acting like it.

Hailey stops near the corner of the building and spins around to face me. Now I see what she was hiding inside. The hurt. The anger. It's written all over her face.

"It was all a lie, wasn't it? Everything between us just one big, fat lie to you," she says, her voice soft but shaking as she tries to hold back the tears.

"No! None of it was a lie. I love you, Hailey. I'm crazy about you. I would never do anything to hurt you, especially cheat on you with another woman and really especially with that food lady Brooke."

Her eyes well up with tears, but she shakes her head like she's willing herself to stay strong and not show me how devastated she is. She doesn't have to worry about that. I know what she's feeling. Her emotions came through loud and clear in her texts.

That's why I rushed over here. I knew she was telling herself I'm just like that asshole she caught cheating on her.

But I'm not.

Hailey falls silent for so long I want to fill up the empty space with more words about how much I would never do what she thinks I did. I hate standing here with her so close but feeling like she's slipping away from me with every second that passes. I reach out to touch her, but she shakes her head and backs away.

Finally, she can't stop her tears from falling and lowers her head to hide her face from me. "I heard the recording, Cade. I heard you talking. It was your voice. I heard you kissing her. I heard it all."

"What recording? I don't know what you're talking about," I say, but it's like I'm watching her drift away as the memory of those few minutes with Brooke pass through my mind.

"I heard your voice! It was you, and you sounded so guilty. You knew what you were doing was wrong. Twice I've known the truth about you with my own senses. I saw with my very own eyes you and that girl up on that bar, but you made me disbelieve what I knew I saw. Now I heard with my very own ears your voice and hers while you and Brooke were together. Are you saying I shouldn't believe that either? Do I have to have all my senses prove what you are? Maybe I should taste another woman on you or smell her on you for proof? Do I need to feel another woman touch you to finally have enough proof that you'll admit the truth?"

Hailey begins to sob, and I know I have to tell her the whole truth. It's now or never. But nothing really happened. She has to understand that. I didn't want to offend Brooke and ruin Hailey's chances that she could really get her to help her.

"Okay, okay. There was a kiss, but I didn't kiss her. She kissed me. I should have pushed her away quicker, but I was worried that if I did anything to piss her off that she'd take it out on you. She came looking for me at the club. I didn't want to see her. She said she wanted to talk about helping you, so I took her into the office. That was all I wanted to do, but when we got in there she obviously had other plans."

I stop myself from saying anything more and try to get Hailey to look at me. She lets me lift her chin, and when she looks up at me, her beautiful blue eyes are all watery. Looking at them breaks my heart, so I have to continue talking so she knows what happened. That I didn't do anything with that woman.

"You have to believe me, Hailey. Nothing happened. I don't know what kind of recording she has, but it's not real if you heard me saying I wanted her or even gave a damn about her. She's the food lady to me. That's it. The person who said she wanted to help you get the word out about all the great things you make."

As tears stream down her face, she stares up at me, tearing my heart out of my chest at seeing her like this. Then she says the words that make me feel like someone's carved into the center of me and left an empty space I won't be able to fill without her in my life.

"I never want to see you again, Cade. Don't text me. Don't come here and stand out in the parking lot waiting for me. Just stay away from me. Whatever I was to you I'm not anymore, so go find some other girl to play with."

Her words stun me, and I reach out to stop her from going back into the restaurant, but she pushes me away. And then she's gone, and I'm left standing there in the midday sun feeling like all the goodness in my life has been taken from me.

TIPPING THE BOTTLE UP TO MY MOUTH, I DRAIN THE last few drops of whiskey and toss it onto the couch next to me. For five hours, I've sat here trying to drown my ability to feel. It hasn't worked. If anything, I feel more, not less about losing Hailey than I did all those hours ago.

I hear the front door open and look toward the hallway to see Alex walking toward me. Not exactly the person I hoped would stop over tonight.

"Hey, what the hell are you doing sitting here? You're supposed to be at work," he says as he sits down in the chair in front of me.

"What are you? A fucking timeclock? Unless you're here to deliver more whiskey, go away."

Alex leans forward and narrows his eyes to look at me. "Are you drunk?"

"Yeah. And I plan on getting even more drunk just as soon as I can find another bottle," I announce before attempting to stand up.

Gravity or drunkenness, whichever is the more powerful force on me at the moment, sends me falling back onto the couch, and I give Alex a shrug. Guess I'm not looking for more to drink right now.

"What's going on, Cade? I've never seen you like this. You're supposed to be at work. Your father called me and asked me to come over here to see if you're home because he couldn't get in touch with you."

I grab my phone and hold it up for him to see. "I got his calls. I got his texts too. Today's been my day for texts I didn't fucking want."

"Why are you sitting here hammered when you're supposed to be at work?"

"Because I fucking hate that place, okay? Hate it!" I yell.

Alex nods like he understands. Of course, he would. He's known me for my entire life, so naturally he thinks he understands my utter loathing for that place.

"I know. You always have. But this isn't like you not to go to work. What's going on here, Cade?"

Focusing on him, I push myself up so I'm sitting. "I've always hated that club. You know that? My father spent every spare moment of his life when I was a kid there. My mother used to take me there so I could see him and we could have a normal family dinner together because he always fucking had to be at the club by six. He couldn't go in at seven. No, it had to be six. As if any of those fucking drunks that go there every night would know the difference if he waited until we had dinner at home together. He didn't even change when Ava came along."

Alex's face twists into an expression of sadness. "I know. I know you hate working there now too."

"But now I have an even better reason to hate it. First, fucking Katelyn...no, I mean Kylie...fuck, I don't know which one it was but whichever twin it was that decided she needed to put on that fucking show the night Hailey came nearly made me lose her. Then that fucking food lady decided to trap me and fucking tape us together. What kind of manipulative fucking bitch does that? And for what? We didn't do anything, but she told Hailey we did. Now she says all her senses tell her the truth about me."

His sadness gives way to confusion, which is written all over his face even before he starts talking again. "Wait. What? What happened with Hailey?"

I hang my head, too drunk and too sad to look at him when I explain. "She broke up with me. Brooke, the food lady who said she wanted to help her, came to the club and when we went into the office to talk about her helping Hailey, she made a move on me. I don't know how, but she recorded the whole thing and then played it for Hailey. And I really don't know how she made it sound like she and I were together. But she did, and Hailey's gone."

"Did you talk to her? Tell her it didn't happen?"

"Of course, I did. She doesn't believe me. Why would she? She saw what happened with the twins, and now she's heard what supposedly happened with that Brooke bitch. I even went over to her hotel to convince her to tell Hailey the truth, but she left already."

"Why would this Brooke woman do that to her? I thought she wanted to help Hailey because she loved her stuff."

"Isn't that the question of the day? I've sat here for hours trying to figure out why food bitch would do that to someone she just met. Nothing makes sense, but then again, I've been blasted for most of that time, so that could be why I can't work out what the fuck made her do that."

"Maybe she's jealous," Alex says, nodding like he approves of that explanation. "She probably doesn't have the talent Hailey has in her little finger in her entire body."

Leaning back, I let my head rest against the couch cushion. I'm tired of trying to figure out what food lady's motive was.

"It doesn't matter why she did it. All that matters is Hailey's gone."

Alex jumps up from the chair and begins moving around the room. That's how he acts when he's excited about something. What he could be excited about in all of this, I have no clue.

"Okay, here's what you have to do. Find out where you can locate this Brooke woman and talk to her. She clearly isn't any friend of Hailey's, and I doubt she has any interest in helping her after what she did to you. Just make her tell the truth and this will all be cleared up. You and Hailey will be back together."

Fuck, he makes it all sound so simple. Or maybe that's just because my drunken mind only understood about half of what he just said.

"It doesn't matter, Alex. It's over. Hailey was right in the beginning. She's not a red Jag girl, and I'm not a guy who deserves someone like her. Karma got me, man. Every woman I've ever been with said this would happen, and lo and behold, it has."

He starts to say something, but I'm too drunk and too tired to listen to anymore. I just want to fall asleep thinking about Hailey and how she'd look at me like she loved me.

Like I could be someone she could love.

CHAPTER NINETEEN

ailey

IN MY BEST EFFORT TO KEEP BUSY AND NOT LET myself think of Cade, I hide out in the kitchen with chocolate and attempt to create something new. The problem is I can't stop thinking of him, and after about an hour, I've eaten more of the chocolate than doing anything else with it.

The air around me smells like pancakes and sausage, the most popular item on the menu every Sunday morning. While the restaurant struggles during the week, Sunday mornings are always a busy time, thankfully. If it wasn't for the breakfast rush each weekend, my parents might have to close the place down.

I peek out the windows in the kitchen doors and

see the crowds have thinned a bit since the last time I looked. Good. That will give my mom and dad a break, to say nothing of the servers and cooks.

As I'm staring out into the dining room, I see a man walk through the front door who catches my attention. Tall with dark hair and a hint of gray at the temples, he's attractive, but I think my mind must be playing games on me because he looks like an older version of the person I'm trying so very hard not to think about this morning.

Or ever again.

Curious, I step out to take a better look. Who is this man? Is it just a coincidence that he looks like the spitting image of Cade?

"Hailey, someone to see you!" Hannah calls back to me.

I walk toward where she stands with him, cautious that I might be going crazy. Too much Cade on my brain.

"Yes?" I say with a smile I hope doesn't show how odd I feel at this moment.

Hannah walks away, leaving me standing in front of this older lookalike of the man I so desperately want to not have on my mind anymore. Is this the universe playing some kind of cruel trick on me? Isn't it bad enough I trusted Cade and he made me look like a fool? Do I really need to see his face in every guy that shows up here?

"Hailey? It's nice to meet you," the man says as he extends his hand to shake mine. "I'm Stefan March, Cade's father."

A nervous giggle escapes from my throat. "I guess what they say is true. You can't plant peas and get corn. You look just like him."

Stefan gives me a big smile and leans in toward me. "I think I get to say he looks just like me since I came first."

"I guess. Yes, that would be right."

"Do you have a few minutes? I'd like to speak to you," he says in a kind voice that sounds so much like his son's it's unnerving.

But I can't talk to him or anyone else about Cade today. It's too soon. My emotions are too raw, too close to the surface, and there's no way I'll get through a conversation with him about his son and not cry.

"I'm not sure that would be a good idea right now."

"Well, then will you let me show you something? No talking. Just showing. I promise it won't take much of your time."

Still unsure if I should even do this, I point toward an open booth on the far side of the restaurant. "Okay. We can sit over there."

Good to his word, he doesn't try to make conversation at all as we walk to the booth. When we sit, he remains silent but sets a laptop on the table.

Spinning it around, he lifts the top and presses a button to light up the screen. "All I ask is that you watch."

I look over the laptop and give him a smile, noticing how similar his deep brown eyes are to his son's. Deep brown eyes that I've looked into so many times and found the calm I needed.

"Okay."

When I look back at the screen, I see a black and white picture. It's a recording of some sort, but I don't know from where or of what.

As if he's reading my mind, Stefan says, "This is the security camera footage of my office from Friday night. The sound will come up in a few seconds."

For a moment, I panic. I don't want to watch this. I can't see Cade with someone else. Why would his father come here to show me that? Is it that he doesn't want the two of us together? Because if that's the case, he didn't have to bother coming all the way over here to show me the video proof his son cheated on me. I already heard the audio.

But then I see on the screen Cade and Brooke standing there in the middle of his office talking, and it's not like she said it happened at all. He's talking about how he hopes she'll help me. He doesn't look like he's interested in her. Everything he's saying is for my benefit.

Then I see her climb on top of him and kiss him, just like he claimed she did. It's only for a second or two, though, and then I hear him say the words any girlfriend would want to hear in this situation.

"Brooke, whoa. I'm with Hailey. She's my girlfriend. I just wanted to get you to help her. You need to get off me. Now."

I stare at the screen as she makes some excuse about why she hit on him, but I'm not listening anymore. All I can see is Cade doing exactly what he told me he did.

Stefan closes the laptop and lets out a heavy sigh after Brooke leaves the office. "Nobody is harder on Cade than I am, but he's a good man. He wouldn't do anything to hurt someone he truly loved, and he loves you. That's obvious. I just thought you should see this since I've been told you heard some version of it that isn't true."

"What did he tell you?"

He shakes his head and smiles. "My son wouldn't tell me anything. We aren't like that. That's my fault, but that's the way it is. His cousin Alex told me after he found him drunk last night when he didn't come into work."

"She told me they were together. She played me a recording with his voice on it saying those words he said on the security tape, but not all of them. She twisted everything to make it seem like they were together."

Stefan nods. "Doctored. Probably just a splice job. It isn't hard to do. If she has someone around her who knows anything about production, it could have been a very convincing version of what happened."

Someone like the production guy she has who helps with her podcast. I've been such a fool! I barely knew her, but I believed her lies over what the man I love was trying to tell me.

I cover my face with my hands, not wanting Cade's father to see me fall apart. "God, I said such horrible things to him. He must be so hurt. I was so angry, though."

"Something tells me it's not too late."

Wiping my eyes, I can't help but feel like it might be. "I wanted so much for Brooke to help me get the word out about my desserts to help my parents keep this place open that I couldn't see anything but that. I feel so foolish, and I've hurt Cade because I wanted to believe her."

"For what it's worth, you did hear his voice on the tape. I don't think anyone could blame you for believing what she told you."

I look down at the table to avoid meeting Stefan's gaze as the real truth becomes clear. "I believed it because it was something I always feared. I always worried I wasn't the type of person he should be with. I'm not really a red Jag kind of girl, as you can tell."

"Well, my son doesn't let his mother or me meet most of the women he dates, but we hear things since he and Alex are so close. Cade's never felt for any of them what he feels for you. That I do know. He even told me about you the other night. He said you went to school for psychology but something made you change your career path to begin baking here for your parents' customers. And from what I hear from my brothers and Alex, they'd love to have your desserts to serve their customers at CK."

He stops and lets out a heavy sigh. "Cade is a lot like me when I was his age. I think that's why we lock horns so often. That and I want him to take over the club so I can walk away knowing it's in the best hands possible and he hates the place. In that way, we're very different. I loved living the life of a single guy until I met his mother. Then, it was like someone suddenly turned on a light and I saw I didn't want to live like that because I wanted her in my life more. I think that's what Cade's found out with you. I'd hate to see him lose that because of someone's malicious attempt to break you two up."

Maybe it isn't too late.

"I need to talk to him. Right now. I'm sorry, Stefan, but I have to go."

I shimmy across the seat to leave, but he stops me. "Wait. I'm tired of being the only one who hasn't tasted one of your creations. Do you have any today?"

"Hang on. I'll be right back."

When I return to the table, I set an apple tart in front of him. "All I could do today was mope over a bowl of chocolate. This was from what I took that awful woman, but I promise it's still good."

"I'm sure it is," he says with a smile so similar to his son's. "Thank you for listening, Hailey. It was very nice to meet you. I think I'm going to enjoy this."

"Thank you very much for coming here to help me see the truth, Stefan. I hope this isn't the last time we meet."

With a shake of his head, he says, "I don't think it will be."

AFTER RACING THROUGH TRAFFIC, I GET TO CADE'S condo in record time after treating stop lights as optional on at least two occasions and the stop sign near his building as more of a glide sign. I run past the people walking in and get into the elevator to take me to the fifteenth floor. A few people getting on two floors up means I have to wait an extra thirty seconds to get to him, and by the time I reach his floor, I'm more nervous than I was the first time I came here.

I knock on his door, but I get no answer. I was in such a hurry to get to him that I forgot to check to see if his car was in the parking lot. He might not even be here.

Disappointed, I knock one more time and wait as each second that goes by I lose hope that I'm going to get to talk to him. I give the door knob a jiggle in a last ditch attempt to get inside, and I'm thrilled when it actually opens.

Rushing in, I look around but don't see him. I hurry into his bedroom, but the bed looks like it hasn't even been slept in. Did he go out and stay somewhere else last night?

The very idea of him licking his wounds over our breakup with someone else makes me feel sick. Disheartened, I walk out to the living room and there on the couch all curled up is Cade sleeping.

I crouch down beside him and press a kiss to his lips. Slowly, he wakes and looks at me like he isn't sure what he's seeing.

"Hailey? What are you doing here?"

"I came to tell you I was wrong. I'm sorry, Cade. I'm sorry I believed her. I'm sorry I said all those awful things to you."

Wide awake after hearing that, he sits up in front of me. "It doesn't matter. You were right. Who I am is the problem," he says sadly.

"No! It wasn't you. I know that now."

Cade sighs and shakes his head. "It's karma. Every single woman I've ever been with said this would happen. Now it has. It's cosmic payback for how I was with them, for who I was before I met you."

I grab his shoulders and shake him, desperate to make him understand. "Stop this! I know what happened with Brooke. Or better yet, I know what didn't happen. I'm sorry I didn't believe you when you told me nothing happened between you two."

"You don't believe her anymore?" he asks, sounding so hopeful that I just want to take him into my arms and hold him forever.

Looking into his eyes, I see hope there too. "No. I saw the whole thing on the security tape from your father's office that night. I know you didn't do anything wrong. I heard what you said to her. You were trying to help me, like you always are."

"How did you see the security tape?"

"Your father. He came to see me at the restaurant this morning to show me. I'm so sorry, Cade. I should have believed you, but that recording sounded so real. It was just my insecurities blinding me to the truth. I should have known it never happened the way she said it did."

Cade sighs, his shoulders sagging in relief. "My father came to see you?"

"Yes. He played the tape from when you and Brooke were talking in his office, and I saw it all. It happened just like you said it did."

"How about that? Just when I think he and I might never get along, he goes and does something like this."

"I thought when I first saw him that he was some kind of memory sent to haunt me," I say, giggling. "You two look so much alike. If that's what your future is, I'm all in. You have good genes."

"Good old Stefan March. Just when you think you know the guy, he surprises you."

I lean forward and press a kiss to Cade's lips as he smiles. "So you forgive me?"

"Of course. I love you, Hailey."

Hearing that, I climb onto the couch to sit next to him, nuzzling my face in his neck. He feels just like he always has next to me.

Right. Perfect. Just where I want to be.

"You know, I drank like a bottle of whiskey last night. I'm sure I smell like the floor of a bar right now."

I take a deep breath in and definitely smell alcohol. "It's okay. I probably smell like chocolate after eating half a bowl of it today. If you're fine with that, I'm fine with you just as you are."

Cade hugs me tightly to him and kisses the top of my head. "I have a better idea. Let's jump in the shower. We can think of it as a fresh start."

"Good idea. We'll wash everything from the past

couple days away and start over," I say as I stand up from the couch.

He gets up and wraps his arm around me. "And we'll have great shower sex because what is making up without that?"

No wonder I love this man.

CHAPTER TWENTY

ailey

THREE MONTHS LATER

My stomach feels queasy like it always does when I'm moving but can't see where I'm going. I know Cade loves surprises, but I just wish he didn't require me to wear a blindfold for them.

"I think I might be sick. I'm just not good with not seeing the road when I'm in a car. I can't even sit in the backseat because I get carsick on trips."

He takes my hand and gives it a gentle squeeze. "Just one block more. If you're really not feeling good, take off the blindfold but keep your eyes closed, okay?"

"That doesn't really solve the problem, but thanks."

I feel the car slow down, and then a few seconds

later, we come to a stop. Thank God. I really don't want to throw up all over whatever the surprise is.

"Okay, just let me come around and open your door. No peeking."

I hear the driver's side door open and feel a blast of hot air enter the car before it disappears when the door slams shut. Then when he opens my door, heat from the outside on this late July day rushes into where I sit. I feel his hand take hold of mine, and I turn to get out of the car.

"Watch your head," he cautions as I slowly stand up and step onto the curb.

"Ready? You can take off the blindfold now," Cade happily announces.

I push it up over the top of my head and see a store's windows in front of me. There's no name on them and no sign above on the building, though.

Turning to look at him, I see Cade beaming a smile. I love that he's so happy, but what's going on here?

"Do you know what this is?" he excitedly asks, clearly not understanding how in the dark I still am, even after taking the blindfold off.

"No. What is it?"

He brings my hand to his lips to kiss it. "This is your new bakery shop. You can still make anything you want for your parents' restaurant, and you'll be able to make all those desserts for CK too. Cassian and Kane told me their customers have been raving about them since you started making them last month, so this will help you do that and anything else you want to do."

I shake my head in disbelief. "You bought me a bakery?"

"Wait until you see it, Hailey. I asked Alex to tell me exactly what you might need for any kind of cake or pie or cookie or pastry or whatever you want to make. Whatever you can create, you have the kitchen to do it. He had one of his friends who's a pastry chef at one of the finest restaurants in New Orleans make a list, a dream list of everything he would love to have in his ideal kitchen, and that along with Alex's ideas is what you have in there. If you can think it, you can make it now."

Happiness fills me, and I start to cry. "You did this for me? How? This must have cost a fortune."

"That trust fund of mine needed to do something other than buy me more stuff I don't need. Seems even though I've been pretty much a loafer this past year, the bank thinks I'm a good risk. Don't worry about how much it cost. Just make whatever your heart desires here and it will all be worth it."

Tears stream down my face as I try to understand someone giving me such a gift. "I don't know what to say."

Cade kisses me and smiles. "Say you love me and you're going to make those incredible desserts and whatever else makes you happy, Hailey."

"I love you, Cade, and when I get over the shock of the man I love buying me a bakery shop, I'm sure I'm going to think up a thousand things I want to try.

I've never had anyone do anything this wonderful for me before."

"Well, I had to do something for our three month anniversary, especially after how great things went with that Jessie woman once she and all her blogger friends found out what Brooke tried to do to you."

"She really was so kind, wasn't she? I still don't understand how anyone found out since you swear you didn't tell anyone."

A sly smile turns up the corners of Cade's mouth. "You do know! Tell me. If it wasn't you, then who?"

"Alex. He's got lots of friends in the food biz, and all it took was telling the right person and the story had legs from there. My best friend is not only a committed hedonist but also someone who likes seeing people get their just desserts."

So it was someone in Cade's family all along. I had a feeling it was, but I couldn't be sure.

"I'd say Brooke Dunning got her just desserts. Jessie says she's practically a pariah in the food blogger world now. Nobody wants to do her podcast these days."

"Good. That's what being a jealous bitch gets her. But enough about food lady."

"You're right. No more talk about her."

"Now that you're making desserts for CK in addition to your parents' restaurant and their business is doing so well because of everything you make, I figured you needed the right kind of kitchen. Plus, when I tell you about the second surprise I have for you today, you're going to understand that this is the least I can do. Trust me on that."

I wipe the tears of joy from my eyes and laugh at how silly he can be. "So what's the second surprise?" I ask, curious how what he has next for me would make me think he needed to buy me an actual top of the line bakery.

"No blindfold needed for that one, although you might tell me later you wish you had to wear one."

"What is it? Nothing can be that bad."

He shakes his head and sighs. "Today, you get to meet the entire March and Jackson family, and by entire, I mean everyone from my cousins to my grandmother and everyone in between."

"And that's a bad thing? I've already met your parents and Alex and Kane, and I guess I technically met Wilder that night out at the island house. How bad could it be?"

He rolls his eyes. "Brace yourself for stories from my childhood and a million questions about us."

I wrap my arms around him and hold him to me. He sounds like he's dreading this get-together today far more than I ever would.

"Well, I for one, can't wait to hear all about you as a little boy. Your mother told me a few things that were adorable. As for the questions, what is there to say about us? You bought me a bakery. I'm madly in love with you. That's the whole story, right?"

"Trust me. My family is going to want to know if we're getting married, where we plan to live, how many kids we plan to have, what their names will be, and a dozen other questions, and that's five minutes after we walk in the door."

This is the first time he's ever mentioned us getting married and doing all those other things. Cade and I have been happier than I thought two people could be after that mess with Brooke Dunning, but neither one of us has ever brought up the word marriage.

Until now.

"Well, what do you want me to say if they ask me those questions?"

He presses a kiss to the top of my head as I look at the front of the bakery he bought me just to make me happy. "Tell them you don't know. It drives the group of them crazy. That's my standard answer for anything, and they hate it."

Looking up at him, I search his face for the answer to the question that's now on my mind. "Okay, but do we know?"

He doesn't answer immediately, and I wonder if he regrets mentioning marriage, even in the way he did. I wait for him to say something, but I feel like I ruined everything by pushing this issue.

"Do you love me?" he asks in a serious tone that makes me nervous.

"Yes."

"And do you believe I love you more than anything in this world?"

"Yes."

A smile lights up his face, making his dark eyes sparkle as he looks down at me like I'm the most important thing in his life. "Then we know. When it's time for them to know, we'll tell them."

He's right. We do know, and what I know more than anything else is I love this man and he loves me.

Everything else is icing on the cake.

Cade takes my hand and brings it up to his mouth in a kiss. "Who knows? Maybe Cash won some big pot in a poker game everyone will want to talk about or Liam finally decided to take that job he's been thinking about for weeks and no one will be interested in paying attention to us today."

I roll my eyes at how cute he can be. "Like the infamous Cade March finally bringing a girlfriend to one of the March family parties isn't going to be the major topic of discussion? I doubt it, but I'm ready."

"Well, let me show you your brand new kitchen before we tackle all of that," he says as he tugs me toward the building's front door.

My brand new kitchen. My brand new bakery.

"Okay, but before I get all tongue-tied and awestruck, I want to tell you something."

"What's that?" he asks, holding up the keys to my new business.

"I love you, and not because you bought me an entire building with a super new kitchen so I can make anything I want. I love you because you're you, Cade."

He smiles, and it's like he lights up from the inside at hearing me say that. "I love you too. Now let's go check out that kitchen of yours. I've been dying to show you this for days, so don't make me wait anymore."

Impatient, he hurriedly opens the door and rushes into the building. "Alex made me promise I'd show you something first, but now that I'm here, I can't remember what it is," he says with a laugh.

I watch him make a beeline for the back of the building and can't help but smile at how happy giving me this gift makes him. Not that I'm surprised. I don't know what other guys with trust funds are like, but Cade doesn't have a selfish or stingy bone in his body.

He turns around and looks at me with excitement flashing in his eyes. "You coming?"

"I'm right behind you!" I yell back as I make my way toward my new kitchen.

How did I ever think for a second I wouldn't fall madly in love with this man?

CHAPTER TWENTY-ONE

ade

I FEEL THE PRESSURE FILL MY CHEST AS I DRIVE UP to my grandmother's house. All the cars tell me everyone in my family is here already.

This will be fine. I'm my grandmother's favorite grandchild. Or at least one of them. I think she might favor Alex a little more since they share a name and I think Alexandria March was a hedonist in her day.

No, this will be okay. It's just me bringing a girlfriend to meet my family. All eight hundred and sixty-two of them. At the same time.

"Cade, are you okay? You haven't put the car in park, and you're squeezing my hand so hard I think the circulation is getting cut off to my fingertips."

I turn to look at Hailey and realize I totally zoned

out from panic for a few seconds there. Opening my hand, I force a smile.

"I'm sorry. I didn't mean to crush your fingers. Are you okay?"

She smiles sweetly, shaking her head. "I'm fine, honey. My hands have gone one-on-one with a mixer and barely won more times than I want to count. I was just worried because you seemed to go blank for a little bit. Are you really that worried about me meeting your grandmother and everyone else?"

Hurt simmers beneath that question, so I quickly move to help her understand why this family get-together is freaking me out. After I put the Jag into park and turn off the engine, I turn to face her and hope I can find the right words.

"It's not you, Hailey. My family can be a lot sometimes, and I'm related to all of these people. I've seen them converge like a pack of hyenas on other girlfriends a few of my cousins have brought to family parties."

Hailey smiles, and I know she thinks I'm exaggerating. I wish I was.

"Hyenas? Cade, they're probably just like your mother and father, and the first time I met them was great. Remember, you were nervous that night too? You were sure your father would make you sound like the world's biggest manwhore and your mother would tell me terribly embarrassing stories about when you were a little boy. Neither of those things happened, and we had a great time. Then Ava and I had a great time together when the three of us went to lunch. This is going to be just like that, I bet."

That dinner with my parents did go pretty well, after all. My father didn't feel the need to play my greatest hits and bring up the name of every woman I've ever dated, and my mother kept her story time to a minimum, sharing only about when I was five and thought people were like dinosaurs and laid eggs instead of giving birth.

But that wasn't my extended family.

"Well, that night didn't include my uncles and aunts, notorious for their questions and gossip more than anyone in the family, except my grandmother. Once Olivia and Abbi get a hold of you, God only knows what kind of information the two of them will wriggle out of you about us. One minute you'll be smiling and explaining how nice you think my grandmother's house is, and the next you'll be inexplicably talking about my favorite place to have sex and how often we sleep together. My aunts are like the CIA, Hailey. And don't even get me started on my uncles."

None of what I'm saying seems to be scaring her, unfortunately. With a giggle, she takes my hand and brings it to her lips in a kiss. "I've never met men who were that gossipy, Cade. I'm sure they're just like your father, and Stefan has been wonderful every time we've spent time together."

I shake my head, wishing I could explain how wrong she is about that. "My uncles are nothing like my father. I love them, but no. They look like they're cool, and Kane has a badass vibe to him that makes it seem like he's quiet and all that, but once their wives are around, forget it. Cassian will be the one to ask when we're going to get married, if his wife or Abbi hasn't first. You'd think it would be my grandmother, but it'll be him. He's got this whole family thing about him, and the thought of adding more people to the tribe practically makes him giddy."

"Well, we already decided my answer is that I don't know, right? I doubt he's going to ask for more than that."

The image of Cassian stepping back all gentlemanly and his wife and Abbi coming in for the second attempt flashes through my mind. I'll probably be talking to Alex about something, and they'll swoop in like vultures with their questions.

Maybe this was a bad idea. We can do this some other time. Maybe in a year or so. Or never. Never works too.

As I reach down to start the car, Hailey leans over and kisses my lips, stopping me. "It will be okay, Cade. I'm sure they're all great people. I love you, and Alex is one of my favorite people in the world after only a couple months now that he and I work together on the desserts for your uncles' restaurant. It's going to be okay. Have some faith."

I close my eyes and let out a heavy sigh. "I just worry that you're meeting people who've known me for my entire life."

"Look at me, Cade."

After I take in another deep breath and let it out, I

do as she wants and open my eyes to see her looking at me like I'm the best thing she's ever seen. "They know all the good, the bad, and the ugly, and even if they don't mean to, I'm worried they're going to make you think you made a mistake."

"A mistake? How?"

"By staying with me after all that happened at the beginning when we first started dating."

She cradles my face and looks into my eyes with that gentle stare that never fails to make me think I'm the luckiest man in the world. "Baby, it was no mistake believing in you. I told you. I don't hold your past against you. Do you know why?"

I shake my head as I realize I don't know the answer to that. I guess I just always assumed it was because she's a good person.

"Because I don't want people to hold my past against me. What if you found out a little over a year ago I was a mess and that made you think you shouldn't take a chance on being with me?"

"It wouldn't."

"Well, for some people it might. People change, Cade. Being around you has brought out a lot of things in me that were hidden for a long time when I was with Malcolm and then after what happened with him. I like that change in me. I think you're a different person too, and even if your family brings up that you've been with a lot of women before me, which I doubt they will, that's okay. Your past is your past. What we have now is our present."

She never fails to make me happy. "And we have our future."

"Exactly. And our future. So don't worry about what they ask when you're not there or that they tell stories about when you were little. All of it just makes me love you even more, okay?"

"All right, but don't say I didn't warn you."

As I move to get out of the car, she says, "You worry a lot for a guy who's so carefree. How bad could these stories be?"

I glance back at her as half a dozen tales of my escapades throughout my life march through my memory. "Remember me mentioning about that woman who's going to at some point walk up to me and slap me across the face?"

"Yes."

"Well, there's at least one other person, probably an old man by now, who would still call the cops on me without even saying hello first. In my defense, though, it wasn't just me. Alex, Cash, and Liam were usually right alongside me causing the trouble."

When I turn away, I hear a tiny giggle escape from her. "I bet you four were just the cutest little hellions this town had ever seen."

"That's not exactly the way we've been described."

MY GRANDMOTHER STANDS IN THE FRONT DOORWAY to her house in white pants and a pale blue top, thankfully alone and not flanked by every member of my family peeking their heads out from behind her. Her ear to ear smile reminds me of how she looked when I first learned how to ride a bike without training wheels.

"Cade! I'm so happy you're here! Come give me a hug and introduce me to this beautiful young woman."

Hailey squeezes my hand for a moment and then loosens her hold. Turning to look over at her, I quietly say, "This is the easy part. My grandmother is going to be the easiest part of this day. Trust me."

We climb the steps to the porch and I open my arms to give my grandmother a hug. "Hi, Grandma. You look great. Did you take up long distance running? Whatever you're doing, don't stop."

She leans back from our embrace and gives me that look of hers that says she knows I'm simply flattering her. "You're just like your father, even if you don't want to think you are. He always knew just how to charm people too when he was your age."

"I'll take that comparison, Grandma."

Looking around me, she smiles. "And who is this beautiful girl in the yellow dress looking like the personification of summer?"

As if she doesn't know all the vital statistics like the back of her hand already.

I reach out and take Hailey's hand to pull her to my side. "Grandma, this is Hailey, my girlfriend. And Hailey, this is my grandmother, the one and only, Alexandria March."

For a moment, she stares at us, and I wonder if I underestimated how she'd react to my not being single anymore. Terror races through me at the idea that right here at the front door we're going to have to deal with the first of many comments about how no one ever thought I'd settle down.

Then she smiles and my stress melts away for the moment. "You are just the cutest couple I've ever seen. You have beautiful blue eyes, Hailey, and I've always been partial to blue eyes since two of my sons have them from my late husband. It's so wonderful to have you here with my grandson. He's probably told you he's my favorite hasn't he?"

Leaning in toward us, she whispers, "He is, but don't tell anyone. Their feelings would be hurt, but how could he not be my favorite? Just look at him."

Not surprising since my father always has been her favorite son. She probably just favors us because we take after her in the looks department.

"So everyone is here already and out back on the porch. They can't wait to meet you, Hailey, but let me give you a little piece of advice. If you just say 'I don't know' to any question they throw at you, they give up relatively soon."

My grandmother turns to look at me and winks. "Isn't that right, Cade?"

"I told her always go with I don't know. It drives them crazy and you don't have to tell them anything."

She nods and gives us a wicked smile. "He learned that from me, you know. A big family means lots of people wanting to know every tiny tidbit of your life. I don't tell them everything, though. You need to keep them in the dark about some things, don't you think?"

Hailey chuckles and looks over at me. "I think

your grandson here takes after you. He prefers the idea of remaining a mystery too."

"It's the only way to be," I say with a shrug. "Once you start giving them details, forget it. Then people start having opinions about your life, and the next thing you know, there's someone explaining how you can't do what you want while you're trying to eat a hot dog and enjoy a cold beer."

My grandmother laughs at that little bit of truth. "Always remain a mystery. It's the secret to how I get away with all I do in this world. Now let's go in, and remember, no matter what we all seem, we love each other in this family."

She turns on her heel and walks into the house before I look over at Hailey and ask, "Ready?"

"I am, and your grandmother is as wonderful as you said she was. I don't know how old she is, but she's sassy, and I love that. I can see her putting someone in their place and smiling the whole time."

We walk inside and I say, "She can tell someone to go to hell and make them thankful she bothered to take the time to mention it."

The sound of my family having a good time outside filters through the house, but all I feel is dread. We can be a lot to handle. I hope it wasn't a mistake bringing Hailey here today.

She gives my hand a squeeze, and I turn to see her smiling. "This is going to be fun. Try to look like you want to be here, Cade."

CHAPTER TWENTY-TWO

$\mathcal{H}$ailey

CADE'S GRIP ON MY HAND TIGHTENS AS WE WALK through his grandmother's house, and by the time we reach the back door to the porch, I worry he might spin the two of us around and bolt before I even get the chance to see another member of his family. I'm starting to worry there really might be a reason I wouldn't want to meet the entire March and Jackson clan.

I lean over and kiss his cheek as he looks out toward the group of people assembled outside. "There's nothing anyone can tell me that would make me love you any less, okay?"

He turns to look at me, and I see genuine concern in his dark eyes. "I hope you mean that because it's about to get tested this afternoon."

"Don't worry. I love you, and I have a feeling after today, I'm going to love you even more. By the way, I think I saw Wilder out there. Can we make a deal that you won't fight him today? I think your grandmother might hate that."

That breaks the tension, and Cade rolls his eyes. "Okay. I promise. Time to meet the family."

"Who's first?" I ask as I glance out and see a blond woman standing next to a redhead with expressions that say they're dying to meet me.

Cade looks out the door and smiles. "My aunts Abbi and Olivia. The blonde is Abbi, and she's married to Kane. Olivia is Alex's mother. I want to say they're both cool, but by the looks of it, they're about to burst from about a million questions. Last chance to leave. You say the word and we're out of here. My grandmother won't care. She'll think it's mysterious."

"It's going to be great. I know the drill. Lots of I don't knows and smiles."

"Brace yourself for so many stories about when I was little from Olivia. I spent a lot of time at their house with Alex."

The dread in his voice is clear, so I kiss him again and whisper in his ear, "It's okay. I don't think she could tell me anything more embarrassing than the story you told me about when you and Alex peed in your sleeping bags because his brother stuck your hands in warm water."

A nervous laugh explodes out of him, and he shakes his head. "You have no idea. Pissing in sleeping bags might be the least disgusting thing Alex and I did as boys. Just remember you love me, okay?"

Before I can tell him I would never forget, I hear a man's voice call out, "Cade, you can't hide in there forever. Come on out and let us meet your girlfriend."

He pushes the door open as he explains, "That's Cassian. He's married to the redhead. He used to be my favorite uncle until about five seconds ago."

We step out onto the porch and Alex greets us with a beer for Cade. "I didn't know what to get you, Hailey, but considering that you two are all my mother and Abbi have talked about all day, I figured a drink would be in order."

"I think I better stay sober today," I joke as Cade tilts the bottle up to his mouth and takes a gulp of beer. "I tend to get a little dopey when I drink."

Alex smiles and reaches over toward the porch railing for a bottle of lemonade. "Understood. Hey, what did you think of the kitchen over at the bakery? Cade said he was going to show you before you came over."

I open my mouth to tell him how much I love all the cool things he insisted should be included in the kitchen, but before I can say a word, Cade's aunts hurry over to say hello. Both beautiful women, I instantly can tell that Olivia is the chatty one and Abbi is a little more reserved.

And like Cade warned, they immediately begin to ask questions about how we met, how long we've been dating, and a dozen other topics, but I've got a plan ready. Standing next to me, Cade tries to interject answers to save me, and he succeeds for a few seconds.

"Abbi and Olivia, Hailey's going to be around for a long time, so trust me, you'll get to know her," he says when they begin to ask about our plans for the future.

Time to change the subject.

While I search my purse for my phone, I ask them, "Did you know Cade bought me a bakery? Want to see pictures?"

And just like that, his two aunts fall silent, their mouths open in shock.

I hold up my phone in front of them and smile at Cade. "Alex helped him decide on what machines he should buy and how it should be set up. Now when I'm making my desserts, I have a brand new kitchen to make them in."

Out of the corner of my eye, I see Stefan walk up the stairs and take a peek at the picture of the bakery. Leaning in, he kisses me on the cheek and whispers in my ear, "That's how you do it in this family. Congratulations on the new business."

As Abbi and Olivia watch Cade scroll through the dozens of pictures I took earlier, I give his father a smile. "I'll make sure one of the first things I do is whip up a batch of those lace cookies you love."

His eyes roll back in his head, and he sighs. "Oh, I do love those. Just tell me when and I'll be there."

"Is Shay here?" I ask before scanning the faces below in the yard.

"She will be later, I hope. Her research has her tied up the last couple days."

Disappointed she isn't here to chat with, I nod. "I wanted to show her the new bakery pics."

Even more, I hoped she would help me with her sisters-in-law.

"It looks like you'll be tied up for a while with these two," he says with a smile, pointing at Olivia and Abbi.

"Ladies, ladies, let Hailey have some breathing room," Cade's grandmother announces a few moments later, probably after her son said something to her on his way inside the house. "She's going to be here with us all day, so let her enjoy her lemonade and relax for a few minutes."

Cade takes the opportunity to whisk me down to the beach as his aunts and uncles talk amongst themselves about the new bakery. Alex follows behind, and we join two men who look very much like the uncles we just walked away from on the porch.

"Hailey, I'd like you to meet my cousin Cash and my cousin Liam. Cash is the redhead's son, and Liam is the blonde's."

The two of them look so much like their fathers that there'd be no way I couldn't figure out they were related. "You guys really do only have two looks going on in this family, don't you?"

Laughing, Cade nods. "You either look like my father or their fathers. Nothing in between."

"Not true," Cash says. "Ava looks like your mother more than Stefan."

They all agree, and I can't help but wonder why Olivia and Abbi's traits don't appear to have moved to the next generation. "So not a single redhead or blonde in the bunch here?"

Liam shakes his head. "Strange, isn't it? I guess red and blond hair are recessive genes, and they were no match for the brown hair with brown eyes on one side and the black hair and blue eyes on the other."

"Maybe it skips a generation," Cade suggests as we all sit down on beach chairs arranged in a circle in the sand.

Alex elbows him, and with a sly smile whispers far too loudly, "I guess we're going to see with you soon, huh?"

And here I thought the aunts would be the ones asking the uncomfortable questions.

Cade looks at me and rolls his eyes before elbowing Alex in return. "First of all, dude, where did you learn to whisper? That kitchen of yours? And second, any redheads will be coming from you and Cash here, not me, and Liam will have the chance at a blond kid. I come from two people with dark hair, remember?"

"I definitely didn't expect to have a conversation about genetics today," I say with a chuckle, leaning back to close my eyes and enjoy the feeling of the sun on my face.

"Just wait," Alex says. "A few more beers and we'll be having all kinds of conversations."

"And Cash will have us betting on who's going to have the redheaded kid," Cade jokes. "I forgot to mention to you that these family get-togethers always end up with him offering some kind of bet."

I open my eyes to see Cash smiling. I can definitely see him being able to charm women with that grin.

"It's all in fun. Right, guys?"

Alex and Cade nod, but when I look to my left at Liam, I see he's checking his phone. His expression grows serious before he looks up at us and smiles.

"My luck is changing for the better, it seems. I got that job as a bodyguard I was waiting to hear about for the past couple weeks. Looks like today's my last day of real freedom, so we better make it good," Liam says.

Like his father Kane, he's not as outgoing as his cousins, but I sense he's got a kind heart under that gruff exterior. Cade mentioned he's been hoping to get this job, so I'm not surprised when the other three men toast their congratulations.

"Hey, everyone, Liam's got good news!" Cade yells up to the rest of the family on the porch. "Tomorrow he becomes a bodyguard to the stars!"

"Don't be an asshole," Liam mumbles. "Now I'm going to have to deal with the million questions from my mother and Olivia."

I can barely stifle a smile when Cade laughs and says, "Exactly! Thank God for you and that girl you'll be guarding because now Hailey and I don't have to be under the microscope today."

As the three of them laugh, Liam turns to me and scowls. "He's a son of a bitch, but I'll let him go on it today since you benefit from my good news."

"Thank you, and congratulations. It sounds like a great job."

He nods and gives me a shy smile. I get the feeling he's got a gentle giant thing going on. Only an inch or two bigger than the rest of his cousins, Liam seems bigger and the perfect bodyguard for whoever he's going to be protecting.

"Is the person you'll be working for famous?"

"Not the way Cade said, but to some people she is. She's a pianist. Her name is Mia."

"Classical pianist? That's impressive."

"Even more impressive is she's young. Not even twenty yet, and she's about to set out on a tour that might end up taking her around the world," he explains.

"Then we need to get this party started," Alex announces as he stands up from his chair. "Refills for everyone, and Hailey, still sticking with lemonade?"

"Maybe I'll have one beer now that the pressure's off."

Alex slaps Cade on the back as he starts to walk away. "She fits in perfectly with us. By day's end, we'll have her playing a game of poker with us."

He turns to look at his brother and smiles. "You brought the chips, right?"

Cash looks surprised at that question. "Do I ever not come ready to play a game of poker?"

Leaning over toward me, Cade kisses my cheek. "Sorry I was so stressed out before. I should have known you'd be great."

"So I fit in, huh?" I ask with a smile.

"Of course. That trick you pulled with the bakery pictures was perfect, by the way. Bold move. I was going to save that news for later, but you shocked everyone right out of the gate."

"Your father gave me that idea. He said he's always found deflection to work best. After the classic I don't know, of course."

Cade's smile lights up his face. "So now that you've won over the entire March and Jackson clan, what's next?"

I glance at Liam and Cash sitting around us before I kiss him. "Well, I hear there's going to be a poker game sometime today, so I need to keep my wits about me for that. There's always the friend of mine who's crazy about your best friend, so I'd like to see if I can help her case with him today. And I'm more than a little curious to know about this young pianist your cousin is going to be doing bodyguard duty for."

"Well, we like to keep things interesting in this family, for sure."

Taking his hand in mine, I bring it to my lips and press a kiss to his fingers. "Then, there's my favorite March, of course, the infamous Cade March, who deserves something incredible after today's surprise. Got any ideas for what that should be for later?"

He thinks for a few moments and then gets a wicked look in his eyes. "Read any great books lately? Maybe we could try something from one of them."

LOOK FOR THE THIRD BOOK IN THE NeXt SERIES, RAVENOUS, THE FIRST BOOK IN CASH MARCH'S STORY!

INFAMOUS EXTRAS

Some scenes don't make it into the final book but still deserve to be read. Happy reading!

K.M.

STEFAN

My eyes feel heavy, so I lean back against the headboard and relax, ready to sleep after a long night at the club. Beside me, Shay shuffles through papers, stacking piles at her feet, on her legs, and between the two of us.

"They really should give you an award for work above and beyond the call of duty," I sleepily say before opening one eye a crack.

She rolls her eyes at my suggestion and stacks more papers next to my right leg. "I need to get these done. My students need to know where they stand, and since this class is accelerated because it's a special course, there's no time to dilly-dally."

I sit up and stare at her until she looks over at me.

"Dilly-dally? You've never once in your life dilly-dallied. Seriously."

Leaning over, she kisses me sweetly on the lips. "Exactly, and this is no time to start."

As much as I'd love to discuss how that's not really an answer that makes sense, I'm too tired to bother now. After work and dealing with Cade, I have little more to say than my question about Shay dilly-dallying.

Right on cue, as if she can read my mind, she nudges my side. "So how did things go with Cade tonight? You said you and he talked, but then you clammed up. What's going on?"

"Clammed up? Dilly-dally? I feel like I've been transported back to the fifties," I say with a chuckle.

Shay gives me a sideways glance and shakes her head. "What would you know about the fifties?"

"I watched Happy Days in reruns when I was a kid. I know a lot about the fifties."

She tosses papers onto the pile at her feet and looks over at me with an odd expression that includes an arched eyebrow of disbelief. "Not that I'm an expert on midcentury America, but I have a feeling watching reruns of Happy Days doesn't really give a person the full treatment on the fifties, Stefan."

"What can I say? It schooled me," I say with a shrug.

"What you can say is what happened between you and our son tonight. How is he handling being back at the club?" she asks, likely knowing all too well how Cade's dealing with that.

I take a deep breath in as I try to come up with a nice way of saying he fucking hates it. I really don't want to get into an argument with my wife tonight.

"He'll adjust. He always does, Shay. He's like you were there. It was never where you belonged, but you owned every inch of it every minute you were in the building."

She squeezes my forearm and leans over to kiss me on the cheek. "I know it was hard what you had to do. It's totally not in your makeup to take away his trust fund, but he needs to understand there has to be some direction to his life. I know you hated doing that, but it's the right thing. That's why I suggested it. We should have done it before this, in my opinion."

"I guess. I just felt like my father when I had to do that to him. Cassian March the second would have done something like that and relished every minute of it."

"That's the difference between you and your father, Stefan. Don't beat yourself up about this. You did this because we agreed he needed a fire lit under him after a year of wandering around like some wealthy playboy."

"I guess. It's pretty much what he expected of me, so it's not like it's completely out of character for me. I'm not exactly his favorite person."

Shay doesn't respond to that. Stacking up all three piles into one, she sets them down on the floor beside the bed and turns to face me.

"You know why that is, don't you?" she asks in that tone that says she thinks I'm being a lunkhead because I can't see something that's as obvious as the nose on my face.

I'm not in the mood for question and answer period tonight, so I simply shrug. Why my son and I are like oil and water has always vexed me. He looks just like me, but it's like we're night and day. No two people have ever been more different, and for the life of me, I don't know why.

"Really, Stefan? You don't know why you two are always at one another's throats over the least little thing?"

She says that like I'm one of her dimwitted freshman students she can't fathom ever making it to graduation. "Really, Shay. I mean, we're like twins, yet I fight with him more than I fight with Kane, and that's saying something. If you know what I don't, enlighten me, please."

Shay taps my arm and smiles. "It's because you're like twins that you two don't get along. He looks like you. He acts just like you. I swear sometimes when I'm talking to him, it's like I'm talking to the Stefan from twenty years ago at Club X."

"That guy was a great guy," I joke, not believing my problem with my son is because we're too alike.

She tilts her head and looks at me. "That guy is Cade. Fun-loving. Good time. Everything is light and easy. How can you not see that?"

"Because I'm still that guy and he's nothing like me. Other than the way he looks, I mean."

"Stefan, our son is so you that I can't believe it sometimes. He has that funny way of being cute one minute and infuriating the next. That's quintessential Stefan March."

Hanging my head, I try to remember when Cade was cute with me. It's been a long time. Not since he was a little boy.

"I don't get that Cade, I guess. Maybe he saves that for you and Ava."

As she turns out the light on her nightstand, she laughs, which only makes me sulk more. "You get the same Cade we do. You just find him frustrating because it's like dealing with another you."

In the darkness, I try to make heads or tails of what she's saying. None of it makes sense. If he was just like me, then we'd get along famously. Two peas in a pod. A father and son team to rival those throughout the ages.

Instead, we spend ninety percent of our time going toe to toe on everything and the other ten percent of the time avoiding one another. Pretty much like my father was with me, when he bothered to pay attention to me, that is.

I never wanted to be like my father. I wanted my son to always know I loved him and would always be his biggest champion. How did we get to a place where the only words we seem to have for one another are filled with anger?

"For the record, I think dealing with an exact replica of me would be a dream. We'd enjoy the same kinds of things, laugh at the same jokes, and get along fantastically."

Snuggling up against my side, Shay whispers in

my ear, "You can trust me that he's just like you, honey. You two don't get along because you refuse to understand each other."

"So it's not just me?"

"No. Cade knocks heads with you because he wants to be his own person, but every time he looks in the mirror, he sees you. Can you understand why that would make him want to be rebellious?"

When she puts it that way, I guess I can sort of understand, even though seeing me in the mirror is a hell of a lot better than seeing many other people staring back at him. He could look like my great-grandfather with his turn of the century dour expression and complete lack of style. Every time I saw pictures of that guy when I was a child, all I could think was life must have been miserable back then.

Into the silence of our bedroom, I ask the question that I've never figured out the answer to, even as I try to understand our son. "Is that why he doesn't want to take over the club, even though I'm more than happy to simply hand it over to him? No muss. No fuss. Just here are the keys and enjoy yourself and all the money you'll make. Because he's a natural at running the place. He's just like you, Shay. He's not there five minutes and he picks out all the issues and sets to solving them."

"He wants to be his own man, Stefan. You can understand that, can't you? That's all you wanted when you were his age. You just didn't have a lookalike father telling you what to do."

True. By the time I was Cade's age, my father was

dead and there were no more chances for us to have any relationship at all.

"Well, maybe I'll give up on him taking over Club X and start to look for buyers. I just didn't want him to miss out on me being able to give him that to get him started in life. That's all."

"Give him some time. You might find that in a couple years, he'll be more interested in that gift. But if he isn't, it isn't a slight against you, Stefan. It's just not who he is."

She kisses me and lays her head on the pillow next to me. "You know, you do have another child. Maybe Ava will want to be the owner of Club X."

A million thoughts, each more horrible than the last, race through my mind about my little girl being in charge of the club. Oh, no. No, no, no.

"You better be joking, Shay, because I swear I'm going to have nightmares now of Ava around the people who frequent the club. I might not get any sleep at all tonight after that."

My wife giggles, amused by the horror she's injected into my brain right before bed. "You know, you weren't such a caveman when it came to females before Ava. Do you forget that? I think you would have had me run the club if it came down to it."

I turn my back to her and punch my pillow to fluff it up. Whoever I was then or now or whenever has nothing to do with my daughter running Club X. Oh, no. Just the thought of the men there slithering up to her and trying out their lines on her makes my stomach twist into a knot.

"Goodnight, Shay."

She wraps her arms around my waist and gives me a gentle squeeze. "Goodnight, honey. Don't worry about the kids or the club. It will all work out. I know it will."

Like always, Shay's asleep in less than a minute, leaving me to stare at the wall in the darkness and try to forget what she said. Better to focus on Cade and that business about us being too alike.

Maybe we are.

KEEP READING FOR THE RECIPES HAILEY USED TO MAKE HER DELICIOUS DESSERTS!

Macarons
Ingredients for 30 macarons
Macarons

- 1 ¾ cups powdered sugar
- 1 cup almond flour, finely ground
- 1 teaspoon salt, divided
- 3 egg whites, at room temperature
- ¼ cup granulated sugar
- ½ teaspoon vanilla extract
- 2 drops pink gel food coloring

Vanilla Buttercream

- 1 cup unsalted butter, 2 sticks, at room temperature

- 3 cups powdered sugar
- 1 teaspoon vanilla extract
- 3 tablespoons heavy cream

PREPARATION

1. Make the macarons: In the bowl of a food processor, combine the powdered sugar, almond flour, and ½ teaspoon of salt, and process on low speed, until extra fine. Sift the almond flour mixture through a fine-mesh sieve into a large bowl.

2. In a separate large bowl, beat the egg whites and the remaining ½ teaspoon of salt with an electric hand mixer until soft peaks form. Gradually add the granulated sugar until fully incorporated. Continue to beat until stiff peaks form (you should be able to turn the bowl upside down without anything falling out).

3. Add the vanilla and beat until incorporated. Add the food coloring and beat until just combined.

4. Add about ⅓ of the sifted almond flour mixture at a time to the beaten egg whites and use a spatula to gently fold until combined. After the last addition of almond flour, continue to fold slowly until the batter falls into ribbons and you can make a figure 8 while holding the spatula up.

5. Transfer the macaron batter into a piping bag fitted with a round tip.

6. Place 4 dots of the batter in each corner of a rimmed baking sheet, and place a piece of parchment paper over it, using the batter to help adhere the parchment to the baking sheet.

7. Pipe the macarons onto the parchment paper in 1½-inch (3-cm) circles, spacing at least 1-inch (2-cm) apart.

8. Tap the baking sheet on a flat surface 5 times to release any air bubbles.

9. Let the macarons sit at room temperature for 30 minutes to 1 hour, until dry to the touch.

10. Preheat the oven to 300°F (150°C).

11. Bake the macarons for 17 minutes, until the feet are well-risen and the macarons don't stick to the parchment paper.

12. Transfer the macarons to a wire rack to cool completely before filling.

13. Make the buttercream: In a large bowl, add the butter and beat with a mixer for 1 minute until light and fluffy. Sift in the powdered sugar and beat until fully incorporated. Add the vanilla and beat to combine. Add the cream, 1 tablespoon at a time, and beat to combine, until desired consistency is reached.

14. Transfer the buttercream to a piping bag fitted with a round tip.

15. Add a dollop of buttercream to one macaron shell. Top it with another macaron shell to create a sandwich. Repeat with remaining macaron shells and buttercream.
16. Place in an airtight container for 24 hours to "bloom"

Credit: https://tasty.co/recipe/macarons

Chocolate Glazed Boston Cream Whoopie Pies
Ingredients
Vanilla Pastry Cream

1 1/4 cups whole milk

1/4 cup sugar

2 large egg yolks

2 tablespoons cornstarch

1/8 teaspoon kosher salt

1 tablespoon unsalted butter, cut into pieces

1 teaspoon pure vanilla extract

Cake Cookies

1 1/4 cups Silvana's Kitchen Gluten-Free All-Purpose Flour

1/2 teaspoon baking soda

1/2 teaspoon kosher salt

1 stick unsalted butter, at room temperature

3/4 cup sugar

1 large egg, at room temperature

2 teaspoons pure vanilla extract

1/2 cup buttermilk

Chocolate Glaze

    4 ounces semisweet chocolate, chopped

    3 tablespoons unsalted butter

    1 tablespoon corn syrup or brown rice syrup

DIRECTIONS

Make the pastry cream

Step 1

In a medium saucepan, whisk the milk with the sugar, egg yolks, cornstarch and salt; bring to a boil over medium heat, whisking frequently. Simmer until thickened, about 1 minute. Remove from the heat and whisk in the butter and vanilla extract until smooth. Transfer the pastry cream to a medium bowl. Press plastic wrap onto the surface of the pastry cream and refrigerate until chilled, about 2 hours.

Meanwhile, make the cookies

Step 2

Preheat the oven to 350° and line 2 baking sheets with parchment paper. In a medium bowl, sift the flour with the baking soda and salt.

Step 3

In another medium bowl, beat the butter and sugar with a handheld electric mixer until fluffy, 3 minutes. Beat in the egg and vanilla. Beat in half the flour mixture, then all the buttermilk, followed by the remaining flour mixture, beating until smooth.

Step 4

Arrange twelve 1/4-cup scoops of batter 2 inches apart on the prepared baking sheets; using an offset spatula, spread the batter into 3/4-inch-thick rounds. Refrigerate for 15 minutes.

Step 5

Bake the cookies for 12 to 15 minutes, rotating the baking sheets halfway through, until a toothpick inserted in the center comes out dry. Let the cookies cool on the baking sheets for 5 minutes, then transfer them to a rack to cool completely.

Make the chocolate glaze

Step 6

In a small bowl set over a saucepan of barely simmering water, whisk the chocolate with the butter and corn syrup until smooth. Let cool slightly.

Step 7

To assemble, arrange 6 cookies flat side up on a work surface. Beat the cold pastry cream with a wooden spoon and spread 3 tablespoons of cream onto each cookie. Top the cream with another cookie. Using an offset spatula, spread the chocolate glaze on top of each whoopie pie, letting it drip down the sides. Before serving, let the pies stand until the glaze is firm, about 1 hour.

Credit: https://www.foodandwine.com/recipes/chocolate-glazed-boston-cream-whoopie-pies

Honey-Peppered Strawberries

Ingredients

Fresh strawberries

Honey

Cracked black peppercorns

(In the story, Alex suggests cayenne pepper, which is a variation on this recipe)

Step 1

Dip strawberries in honey and roll in cracked black peppercorns.

White Chocolate Torte with Chocolate Morsels and Raspberries

Ingredients

For the Crust

- 1/3 cup (75g) unsalted butter, melted
- 2 and 1/2 cups (250g) gingernut biscuits/gingersnaps crumbs

For the Mousse

- 3 and 1/2 cups (600g) white chocolate, coarsely chopped
- 1 cup (240g) Greek style yogurt
- 4 gelatin leaves
- 2 and 1/2 cups (600ml) heavy cream, whipped to soft peaks
- Raspberries and chocolate chips, to garnish

Instructions

For the Crust

1. Grease the base and sides of a 9-inch spring form pan. Set aside.
2. Mix together the biscuit crumbs and melted

butter. Press the crumbs into the prepared pan, and chill whilst preparing the filling.

For the Mousse

1. Add the white chocolate to a large microwave-safe bowl, and heat in 20 second intervals, stirring after each one, until melted and smooth. Allow to cool slightly.
2. Place the gelatin into a heatproof bowl. Add 4 tablespoons of cold water and soak for 10 minutes until soft, then place in the microwave and heat until dissolved.
3. Stir together the melted chocolate and yogurt. Stir in the gelatin, then fold in the whipped cream.
4. Pour the mixture over the biscuit crumb base, and spread out evenly. Chill for at least 4 hours or overnight.

Credit: https://marshasbakingaddiction.com/white-chocolate-torte/

ABOUT THE AUTHOR

K.M. Scott writes contemporary romance stories of sexy, intense, and unforgettable love. A New York Times and USA Today bestselling author, she's been in love with romance since reading her first romance novel in junior high (she was a very curious girl!). Under her Gabrielle Bisset name, she write paranormal and historical romance. She lives in Pennsylvania with a herd of animals and when she's not writing can be found reading or feeding her TV addiction.

Be sure to visit K.M.'s Facebook page at **https://www.facebook.com/kmscottauthor** for all the latest on her books, along with giveaways and other goodies! And to hear all the news on K.M. Scott books first, sign up for her newsletter today and be sure to visit her website at **http://www.kmscottbooks.com**

Notorious (NeXt #1)

Infamous (NeXt #2)

If I Dream (Corrupted Love #1)

If You Fight (Corrupted Love #2)

If We Fall (Corrupted Love #3)

Corrupted Love Trilogy Box Set

Crave (Addicted To You #1)

Adore (Addicted To You #2)

Shatter (Addicted To You #3)

Claim (Addicted To You #4)

Addicted To You Series Box Set

In The Darkness (Project Artemis #1)

After The Storm (Project Artemis #2)

Behind The Scenes (Project Artemis #3)

Project Artemis Box Set

Hard Work (Finding The One #1)

Big Love (Finding The One #2)

Sweet Things

Private Secretary

K.M.'S BOOKS ARE IN AUDIOBOOK TOO!